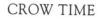

CROW TIME

BOOKS BY SHEILA CUDAHY

Poems (1962)
Clod's Calvary and Other Poems (1972)
The Bristle Cone Pine and Other Poems (1976)
The Trojan Gold (1979)
Nectar at Noon (1989)

Sheila Cudahy

Crow Time

New American Fiction Series: 32

LOS ANGELES
SUN & MOON PRESS
1995

Sun & Moon Press
A Program of The Contemporary Arts Educational Project, Inc.
a nonprofit corporation
6026 Wilshire Boulevard, Los Angeles, California 90036

This book was first published in paperback in 1995 by Sun & Moon Press
10 9 8 7 6 5 4 3 2 1
FIRST EDITION

Some of these stories previously appeared in *The Beloit Fiction Journal,
Fathoms, Furious Fiction, No Roses Review,* and *The South Florida Poetry
Review.* The author wishes to thank the editors of these journals.

This book was made possible, in part, through an operational grant from
the Andrew W. Mellon Foundation, through a production grant from the
National Endowment for the Arts and through contributions to
The Contemporary Arts Educational Project, Inc.,
a nonprofit corporation

Cover: *Two Crows Chewing the Crow,*
photograph by Scott D. Christopher
Cover Design: Katie Messborn
Typography: Guy Bennett

LIBRARY OF CONGRESS CATALOGING IN PUBLICATION DATA
Cudahy, Sheila [1920]
Crow Time / Sheila Cudahy. — 1st ed.
p. cm—(New American Fiction Series: 32)
ISBN: 1-55713-202-X
1. Women—Social life and customs—Fiction.   I. Title. II. Series.
PS3553.U27C76   1995
813'.54—dc20
95-13554
CIP

Printed in the United States of America on acid-free paper.

To

Jenny
  with love to grow on

Charles Simic
  with admiration and thanks

Contents

Crow Time 🐦

REMEMBER our weekend visit in November – Marsha and I brought the kids along as granny bait hoping to lure you to town with us but even that scheme failed to budge you.

"I'll stay on like the crows," you said, and with eyes the color of the Atlantic scanned the Maine shore edged with shuttered cottages, their owners gone. I was so furious I'd have turned around and driven straight back to the city but we'd just arrived and I wasn't going to give in to you so easily or to Marsha's silent "I told you so. Your mother isn't going to budge."

"Crows don't migrate," you continued. "They stay the winter. When the heavy snow falls in December, that old crow in the pine keeps me company."

Timmy and John, believing he did, whined to wait until the black bird flew down and cawed for food at your window. The whines turned to tears on Sunday when we left.

You hurried us home to the city as if we were summer people, not kin who wanted you to come, at least for the worst of the winter. You must have noticed that we left worried and also annoyed. Your stubborn "I'll stay" meant you expected us to return in December.

"Your mother's annual Christmas con," Marsha complained on the long drive back up north that December for the holiday.

As you have pointed out frequently, Marsha's always been a city person, ill at ease in an empty landscape, the trees bare as skeletons against an empty sky.

When we reached Maine the boys nagged me to stop on the side of the road. They wanted to pee in snow they had never seen so much of, so purely fallen, steeping the countryside, blocking your door with drifts left undisturbed until we tramped clouds of silver pollen across the threshold and, bearing gifts and cheer, found you seated in a kitchen chair, head back, eyes staring as if you still could see us with only the whites. The boys ran to the window, excited to discover a few crumbs on the ledge. When the crow refused to come, then they cried.

I trust you appreciate how precisely I followed your instructions the next afternoon, just two days before Christmas it was, when I scattered your ashes under the pine. There seemed to be so few of them, and those few fine as flour on the snow.

"What's daddy doing?" the boys asked in chorus.

"Your father is putting food out for the birds."

The explanation was probably close to what you had

in mind, but her sounding as if I were some crank feeding pigeons in a city park enraged me, and you heard me snarl, "Go wait in the car, the three of you."

On the way home I snarled again, "Get out of the car," and pulled over to the side of the road. "Everybody out."

Nobody moved. "I wanna go home" from the back seat. "Where are we? I don't believe this" from the front.

"Out."

The flat, left rear right down to the rim, was a mixed blessing, the kind you're so good at. I had no time to brood while I took the unopened presents from the trunk to get at the jack – an electric blanket for you from Marsha and me, a thermos from the boys, and their special gift, a ball of suet to hang on the tree – I had no time to brood when I wrenched my back struggling with the iced lug bolts. Even today, after a year, I get an occasional jab of pain, just a reminder – but you ought to know I don't need reminding, especially on a December afternoon like this when it's snowing on the plastic snowballs that decorate the public trees and on the Santas at every street corner stomping their boots in dirty slush mixed with salt as I pass, stepping carefully on the slippery sidewalk.

"My mother phoned," Marsha informs me when I walk in the apartment. "She wants us to come and bring the boys."

I said, "No way," as nicely as I could.

As a rule, I leave the decisions involving her family to her. She is an only child and her parents, lonely and bored since moving to Florida, are very dependent on her.

"This Christmas we're going to stay put," she says.

She has already made her point. The tree has been up for a week, and in the steam-heated living room is beginning to shed a few needles on the rug.

"So she and Dad are coming here. Timmy will have to move in with John. We'll be dreadfully crowded, but that can't be helped."

I agree it can't be, and stare out the living room window. Cars clog the uptown streets with rush hour traffic headed for the suburbs but I am way ahead of them, racing far far beyond the glow of the skyline to where coast, ocean and night sky lie close like enormous aquatic animals sheltering one another.

And here I am, aching back and all, standing under the pine, scattering bird seed. I hope you're surprised. Don't think you've conned me, because you haven't. I wanted to come, always, every Christmas. You've got to believe me so I can go back to Marsha and the boys. There's no rush, though. I won't be hurried away like some intruder.

This place is beautiful: the unblemished whiteness, seeds skittering on the surface like bits of quartz, and fixed against the flux and drift the winged blackness. I wish I could stay on, but it's late, so I'll be leaving.

"Dark outlasts the light," the crow caws.

Christmas People ✏

As I watched them from my bedroom window I knew they were the most beautiful people I would ever see in my whole life, so beautiful that as much as I wanted them to be part of my life, I wondered what I had to offer them.

They walked in silent procession up the flagstone path to the dark house next door. An adult couple followed by three tall boys, a girl who seemed about my age and loveliest of all, a little boy who, as exuberant as the others were restrained, ran back and forth tugging at one and then another. Their faces were suntanned a warm, ripe color and they all had smooth silver-blond hair that rippled in the dusky November light with the motion of their steps, all except the little boy who had tight, golden curls.

"What a strange hour to be moving a big family into that dreadful old house. It hasn't been occupied since before you were born," my mother said, joining me at the window.

"I'm glad we'll have neighbors. Maybe they'll fix up the place," I said.

The house, a tall structure of gray stone set back from the dirt road, stood on a slight rise of what had once been lawn. A covered porch embraced the lower façade, its balustrade and arches decorated with wrought-iron gingerbread. A steep slate roof, several brick chimneys and a windowless tower at one corner added to the building's height.

The house was strange, so out of place in the countryside, it looked as if it might have been lifted, in spite of its bulk, by a gigantic storm and dropped next door.

"Let's hope they're civilized. You know how your father is," my mother sighed.

I knew. He wanted his idea of peace and quiet. As a result, we lived on the edge of town, not a girl my age for miles, nothing but the quiet of empty fields.

"The girl looks to be about your age." My mother sat down on the window seat and leaned forward, squinting. "Maybe you'll be friends," she mused in her unfocused, careless way that usually made me feel non-existent. But this time instead of evaporating I said in my head, "Not just friends. We'll be best friends."

The leaders of the procession had reached the porch steps. Shadows spilling out of dead windows met them.

"The little one with the curls looks out of control," my mother noted, on the alert for anything that might disturb peace and quiet. "Is it a boy or a girl?"

"A boy," I said. "He's beautiful."

The girl picked him up and with the others they disappeared into the empty house.

Next morning, in spite of the bleak weather, I hurried out early to the place nearby on the dirt road where the school bus made its first stop. The girl was already there. She was wearing a blue cotton dress, pale and thin from many washings and a navy-blue blazer that had the worn look of a hand-me-down.

"I'm Susan from next door," I said, coming up to her.

"Ellen Caswell." Shivering slightly she gave me a cold hand.

"Don't you want to get a sweater? The bus is always empty. This is its first stop. I'll get the driver to wait."

"I'm okay." She stiffened her shoulders against more shivers.

"At this time of year, the weather is crazy. I mean, it gets really cold."

"What about snow?" she asked, fixing me with blue eyes under silver-blond bangs.

I could see that snow was important to her.

"Lots in big drifts." I raised my hand above my head to impress her.

She seemed puzzled. "You mean like sand dunes?"

The only sand dunes I had ever seen were in *Lawrence of Arabia* but not wanting to disappoint her I answered, "Yes, only the drifts are blazing white. They sparkle with diamond crystals so bright you have to screw up your eyes."

"Great, real snow, not that horrible fake stuff we always had where we used to live."

I had questions I wanted to ask her like what they used the horrible fake stuff for but the bus came and while we sat together Ellen said, "Mark, my little brother and I have snow dreams," and then she stared silently at the countryside as if trying to visualize diamond-studded drifts.

In November the pastures turn a grayish green, the grass is flattened in yellow patches where white-tail deer have lain to escape the wind. The landscape remains dull most of the winter. We may have some snow in December, enough to cover the ground until it melts into mud or is washed away by chilling rain. Dunes of snow are rare, too rare to fulfill snow dreams.

"Of course, some winters are crummy. Nothing but sleet," I said to reduce expectations, but Ellen wasn't listening. She was talking to herself and to Mark.

"A snow Christmas."

"Class, please welcome Ellen Caswell," Miss Weston, our homeroom teacher, announced when we had taken our places, Ellen at the desk next to mine. She met the welcoming applause with a distant smile.

"Now, suppose you tell us something about yourself," Miss Weston said.

Ellen stood up and after smoothing her lovely hair away from her tanned face said calmly, "Thank you. I am glad to be here. My favorite subject is religion." She sat down.

I figured she had dealt with telling about herself before. In fact, on the way home on the bus that afternoon, she volunteered the information that she had attended a lot of schools.

"All in hot countries. We move around a lot but now

that someone has died and left us the house, maybe we'll stay."

"I hope so," I said.

We got off the bus together and for the first time in my whole life, now that I didn't have to walk home alone, I didn't hate the walk. We walked side by side and came to Ellen's house first.

Thin smoke curling out of one of the several chimneys on the steep roof was the only sign of life.

"See you tomorrow," I said as she started up the flagstone path, but I got no answer. She was already home.

The next morning, Ellen arrived at the bus stop wearing her rope-sole shoes and over her cotton dress a khaki parka so large it came down to her knees. Its bulk made her look more fragile than ever.

"My snow coat. I found it in the attic." She pointed proudly to the old-fashioned metal clasps.

That day the weather turned unseasonably warm. Ellen ignored the change. In class, seeing the parka, Miss Weston smiled. "You certainly are prepared for the cold."

Ellen nodded and pulled the hood over her head. Everybody laughed. The coat from the attic proved to her that all my promises were true. She was ready for real snow.

In the days that followed, I had hoped Ellen would tell me more about herself and her family. An only child, I imagined family life as a wonderful game, a loving circle where stories would be told and secrets kept forever and ever. However, although Ellen and I always sat together on the bus, I learned little beyond the fact that she loved her baby brother, Mark, "more than anyone else in the world, almost more than God. He's four-and-a-half, no longer a baby but we all spoil him, I most of all."

Her face glowed under the fading suntan whenever she spoke of Mark.

"Spoil him how?" I asked.

"Oh, at this time of year I let him play in the infant's crib, take his nap there."

"The infant's crib?"

"Jesus' crib. Every Christmas Eve we lay him in it with fresh straw. Carla, my mother, made him. She and Rolf – he's my father – are artists."

She had a soft, whispery voice and sometimes pronounced or accented a word incorrectly. "Coinci-dánce, nativitée." As a result, I had to listen intently to what she said.

When she noticed that I was as confused about the crib as she had been about snow drifts she added, "On December thirteenth – St. Lucy's Feast, her name means light and she puts oranges in good children's shoes. The naughty ones get coal. Anyway, on the night of her feast day we have a dress rehearsal with the Holy Family. You'll see."

I didn't see but December thirteenth wasn't all that long away so for the moment I asked no more questions, especially because Ellen always kept a certain distance. Part of her was elsewhere. I hoped that as our friendship grew, she would let me in.

Ellen became very popular with the other girls in the class, not that she made any effort to be liked but, in no time, girls were wearing oversized sweaters and parkas over summer clothes.

Finally, without my asking, she talked about her life in the hot countries where she claimed to have lived in houses with thatched roofs and walls open to the sea. When she said she knew how to cook sea urchins and how to avoid jungle head hunters armed with blow pipes, I suspected she was pulling my leg but I had stretched the truth about snow drifts so I pretended to believe everything. In addition, I didn't dare express any doubts for fear she wouldn't want me as a friend.

One day at lunch in the school cafeteria, when we had a table to ourselves, she began to tell about the wonderful times she and Mark had had playing together when he was still a baby.

"Best of all, our *nacimiento* was famous. People came by boats and down out of the hills, entire families bringing wild flowers and fruit, even tiny parrots in wicker cages. We released them as soon as the people left. All gifts for Mark, that is baby Jesus, in the crib. Some pilgrims really believed Mark was baby Jesus."

"You mean you put Mark in the crib to play Jesus?"

"That was before he grew. He still wants to play the part but last year we had to cover most of him with straw. Now we have explained to him that he's too big for an infant."

Ellen interrupted herself in order to go back for seconds. School food didn't bother her. She always had seconds of everything – macaroni and cheese, tuna casserole, milk, bread, jello, apples – and while she didn't wolf her food, she fixed her attention on her plate until she had finished.

"This year Carla has made a statue modeled after Mark when he was a baby. He's very jealous of it but I'll comfort him when the times comes."

"But how do you do it, the *nacimiento?*" I asked, still mystified.

"Oh, they come with us everywhere, St. Lucy, Caspar, Balthazar, Melchior and Jesus, Mary and Joseph."

She spoke as if they were all kin, a traveling family, but it occurred to me that the only member of the *nacimiento* I had seen enter the house that first afternoon had been Mark.

"They travel very easily, the way they first came overseas from Spain, you know, just their heads and hands."

I sure didn't know but hesitated to ask for fear of interrupting her.

"You'll see and with real snow it will be so beautiful."

At the bell, Ellen gulped down her second chocolate milk and we went to math class.

As the weather turned increasingly cold, Ellen asked, "What about snow? When?"

Her "when?" felt like a fist to my gut but I smiled and answered knowingly, "It's too cold to snow now," which was true but when she wrinkled her nose in disgust, I went on hoping to distract her.

"When it does snow, we all go sledding down Hamond's hill. My mom has a big metal tray. You can ride with me."

Although I could remember there being enough snow only twice the experience had been so exciting that now, as I talked, the wild floating feeling returned. I had opened my mouth to the spray. The bright air pressing into my lungs had lifted me into a silver-white cloud.

"It's fantastic. You'll see," I concluded.

Ellen shrugged and sank into the parka. To her, snow was part of a sacred scene, the Holy Family gathered close. Sledding down a hill on a metal tray didn't interest her.

One morning while waiting for the bus, I thought I smelled snow.

"What does it smell like?" She imitated me sniffing the frigid air.

"Kind of wet."

She peered at me with her blue eyes through the darkness and asked impatiently, "What else?"

"Like a wet sheepdog." I figured she couldn't have met, let alone scented such an animal in the hot countries but she had.

"There it smelled musty," she said.

"Here in the cold countries it smells like snow," I answered quickly.

Then we both squealed with laughter and linking arms, jumped up and down to keep warm until the bus came.

That afternoon when I came home my mother said, "You're very cheerful these days. Things must be going well at school."

She wandered past me down the front hall in the direction of the kitchen.

"Have you seen my glasses?"

"No," I answered, going back to my old sullen voice. I wasn't about to tell her that I had a real friend.

I looked forward to Ellen's coming to my house, maybe after Christmas when she wasn't so busy with the Holy Family, and maybe she would invite me to hers. Carla and Rolf sounded really nice. However, my parents (following Ellen's example, I called them Marge and Jake, but only in my head) were anything but friendly toward "those people in that big dark house." Not that the Caswells did anything bad. Rolf had been seen crawling the length of the roof.

"He'll break his neck," Jake had growled. "Those old slates won't hold."

Rolf didn't break his neck. He did disappear. The Caswells were not only silent, they were invisible.

"They're there, by God," Jake would say, seeing a plume of smoke from one of the chimneys. "The whole damn family, but who knows what they're up to."

The closer Ellen and I grew the more I felt the pressure, as if every single Caswell, especially little Mark, were leaning on me to lure the white crystals from the sky into vast jeweled snow dunes in time for St. Lucy's Feast and Christmas. I followed the weather reports in the paper and on TV. They spoke of "coming winter conditions," which meant anything from a freezing storm to instant slush. I thought snow, prayed snow, dreamed blizzards and avalanches only to awaken to windy mornings all blustery and a sky full of clouds chasing one another from one pole to the other and back again but shedding not one flake.

"I hope we have a white Christmas," my mother said one Sunday afternoon.

She had just come in from a walk in the woods.

"Just enough snow for Santa," she added, indulging as she sometimes did in the reverie that "we" were both still very young.

I was, as usual, looking out the window, in this instance out the bay window in the living room when I noticed the blackgarbed figure of Dr. Butler hurrying up the flagstone walk to the Caswell house.

"What's he doing over there?" I asked.

"Just paying a courtesy call. He'll stop by here for coffee afterwards."

"After what?"

"Inviting them to join the church."

"They won't," I said, without knowing exactly why and headed upstairs.

The second floor landing outside my bedroom was an ideal observation post. Dr. Butler sat opposite my mother at a small table in the living room. I recognized him as the pastor of the Episcopal Church of the Incarnation. We went to church off and on, mostly off. My father resented the building's need for repairs. My mother declared she could pray equally well in "God's own cathedral," the pine woods behind the house. Nevertheless, she followed the church's activities and always contributed to the jumble shop.

"You must be chilled to the bone," she said, handing the Reverend a cup of coffee.

He nodded and as he sipped the hot coffee, his Adam's apple bobbed in his stringy neck.

I felt sorry for him. Bones were all there was of him to be chilled. With his small, thin face and tufts of thin hair, he peeked out of his collar like a chick from its nest. Although he was young, he had a deep, hoarse voice like that of an old man. He could make sin sound very scary.

After some chitchat about the church roof, my mother asked with an edge of impatience to her voice, "What did you make of the Caswells? I have tried to make contact with her but she didn't welcome it."

"Hmm," Chilled Bones murmured. "They seem a very self-sufficient, closely-knit family."

My mother bombarded him with questions in no logical sequence. He answered evasively.

No, they probably wouldn't attend services in town. Yes, they are Christians devoted to the infant Jesus.

"They're not Catholics?" she asked anxiously.

"You're thinking of the infant Jesus of Prague. No, their devotion is to the Christmas child. They are serious about the Incarnation."

In his basso profundo the words sounded like a rebuke. My mother ignored it and said, "That house is always so dark."

"Yes, dark and cold. They live and work in the back."
"Work?"
"On a project. Mrs. Caswell said it was the children's

idea some years ago and she encouraged them. It holds them together no matter where they are."

I held my breath. While I didn't fully visualize what was planned for St. Lucy's Feast day and Christmas, I cherished what Ellen had told me as a precious secret between us.

When questioned further, Dr. Butler changed the subject. "Mrs. Caswell was distracted. The little boy misses the tropics and living out doors. He has a bad cough. His sister was trying to keep him quiet."

He went on to praise Ellen which pleased me no end and when he had finished my mother remarked, "She is a close friend of my daughter, Susan."

"Oh, really," he said, putting down his coffee cup. "Ellen never mentioned that she knows Susan."

At that moment the hurt was so sudden, so numbing that I was unable to move. Then, pained and angry, I rushed to my room and closing the window blind, shut out the view of the house. However, by night time I repented and having convinced myself that Ellen shared my desire to keep our friendship a secret for now, I opened the blind.

The sky was full of stars. In their light, the gray stone of the house took on the color of tarnished silver. I knelt on the window seat and closing my eyes, prayed. It was no longer a question of white flakes falling out of the sky. God had to understand that Ellen expected a new, pure landscape of dunes and sparkling crystals as a setting for the Holy Family. I dozed off imploring St. Lucy, whose feast was the next day, to help.

Ellen didn't appear at the bus stop that morning. In recent weeks she had missed several days of school because Mark had been sick.

"I'm the only one who can quiet him down. Everyone else is busy getting ready for the night of the 13th," she told me. She would be especially needed this day.

As I walked to the bus stop alone, I was relieved not to have to face her with her faith in my promises, her talk about the *nacimiento* and a lot of spiritual stuff that made me feel guilty.

My prayers had failed totally. The sky, solid with low clouds, lay like a frozen lake of murky water.

At school, the hours dragged. Miss Weston had the local respiratory bug. She and the radiator at the back of the room coughed and wheezed together. Without Ellen, I spent recess wandering up and down the corridors alone. At lunch I ended up at a table with strangers, little kids who laughed at such stupid jokes and made such disgusting noises that I fled out into the fresh air. In the parking lot, the yellow buses rested peacefully under a dead sky. The air was heavy with moisture. Then slowly, silently, it began. Big wet flakes spiralled down like white moths to die on the black asphalt.

"Snow," I shouted and raced around in a circle with my mouth open.

"Snowing, snowing," little kids yelled, rushing out of the building.

They chased after me, bouncing along in their bright snowsuits like balloons trying to take off. A roar from the parking lot joined our voices. Streams of exhaust poured from the rear ends of the buses as they drove toward us.

By the time my bus reached my stop, the gentle flakes had become clouds of stinging crystals driven by the wind. They swirled out of the darkening afternoon sky, creating their own strange mauve light. I trudged along the middle of the road to avoid the drifts already forming on either side. Opposite the Caswell house, I halted, and protecting my eyes with both hands, saw a single light burning over the front door. Its pale beam barely reached through the darkness to the pointed archway that formed the porch entrance. My eyes watered in the cold, blurring my vision of figures that moved to and fro. One figure, shorter than the others, had to be Ellen.

"Snow, Ellen, snow for St. Lucy tonight," I called as loud as I could, but if Ellen was there on the porch, she didn't answer me.

I ran the rest of the way home.

"You must be chilled to the bone," my mother said.

She was at her desk sweeping her Christmas card list from the rolodex. The deceased, the moved, and otherwise out-of-touch lay in a small pile of cards on the edge of the desk.

"I'm okay," I answered, chilled to the bone.

In my room, I settled on the window seat with pillows and blankets ripped off the bed.

The snow-filled air seemed to bring the house closer, but all I could see of the porch was the one dim light over the front door. Now nothing moved. Then that light went out leaving only a blacked-out hulk.

"I'm too late, I've missed the rehearsal," I groaned and slumped back under the blanket.

Suddenly a blinding light filled my window. The Caswell house seemed to explode. The stone facade, the windows, the roof all flamed in the illumination of tiny gold lights. In their brightness, the snow flakes swarmed like bees. St. Lucy, in a silver robe, looked down from the top of the tower. The porch remained in total darkness.

Still hoping to catch sight of Ellen, I opened the window. A voice – that of a man – called, "Now." Beneath the pointed archway of the porch garlanded with pine boughs and gold and blue lights, stood Mary and Joseph with heads bowed, their eyes fixed on the crib at their feet where the child lay in fresh straw. In Mary's robe I recognized the same blue cotton of Ellen's dress, but under the lights, it fell in folds rich as velvet.

"Mom, hurry. Come see," I turned and called.

"Coming," she answered over the TV.

When I looked out again, there was nothing to see, only the dark hulk in ever deepening drifts.

"See what?" she asked from the doorway.

"Oh nothing much, just the snow." I shut the window.

"Isn't it lovely? I just love being snowbound. Your father phoned. He'll come along after the snow plough." She came and sat beside me. "We can eat in front of the fire and talk about Christmas plans."

"Sure," I said and pushed the blanket aside.

"Those dreadful boots." She pointed at my scuffed hiking boots.

"They're just now getting broken in."

"One day soon I'll pick you up from school and we'll go shopping in the mall."

Marge in the mall was more than I could handle at the moment.

"The Caswells don't believe in presents. Carla, Ellen's mother, says we should be like the Holy Family."

I had hit a nerve. She jumped up from the window seat.

"All right for you, Susan, with your spiritual friends." She glared out the window. "The holy Caswell family." Then in a loud, angry voice she said, "Food stamps." Receiving no reply she repeated even louder, "Food stamps," and left the room.

I felt awful. It had never passed my mind that Ellen was poor. Now I remembered how she had kept her cool when some of the girls had teased her about her dresses and oversized shirts – "hot country," hand-me-down clothes – all the while she complained about the lack of real winter. Now we had real winter and except for that old parka, she had no warm clothes or foot gear.

I changed from my hiking boots to last year's Christmas present, a pair of never worn, nerdy après ski.

Marge had made a beef burgundy for Jake, my father, and after leaving a casserole for him in the warming oven, she and I had a cozy snowbound supper in front of the living room fire.

"I'm sorry, I didn't mean I don't want to go shopping with you," I said.

"Good. We'll go Thursday," she replied and spent the rest of the meal worrying about what to get Jake for Christmas. "I saw a good looking pair of swimming trunks in Gump's catalogue," she mused.

"How about a snowblower?"

Her "hmm" wasn't funny.

After supper I cleared the table and took two oranges out of the fridge.

The air was so cold it took my breath away as I struggled through the drifts on the road to the Caswell mailbox. The weather had cleared. A pale moon shone through the last clouds. In its light, the snow-covered land glowed so intensely that for a moment I thought it must be hot with the white heat of Arabia. Then my lungs cramped. I stuffed a card "To Ellen From St. Lucy" and the hiking boots, each containing an orange, into the mailbox.

When I got back to the house, Marge was glued to a re-run of "I Love Lucy." Now I really was chilled to the marrow and exhausted as well. After a hot bath, I curled up under a pile of blankets on the window seat. Although it was only seven o'clock, I was drowsy. Through half-closed eyes I could see Mary and Joseph bent over the crib. The straw glistened in the moonlight. Just beyond the crib, a tiny foot and pink thigh poked up out of the snow. They hadn't been there before. The straw stirred and Mark lifted his beautiful head, his golden curls trailing bits of straw. Then he fell back out of sight.

"Ellen has spoiled him," I thought sleepily and was about to close my eyes when I heard a sound like waves breaking. Enormous white sprays crested in the flood-lights as the plough slowly worked its way heaping great piles of snow on both sides of the road. The sound must have reached the Caswell house as well for Ellen, wearing a faded night shirt, suddenly appeared on the porch. She hesitated under the arch and, beside Mary, leaned over the crib.

I opened my window but before I could call to her I heard her say, "Mark, where is baby Jesus?"

Mark leapt out of the crib and dressed only in pajama bottoms, dashed off the porch to run tumbling, laughing in the snow, daring Ellen to catch him. Ellen slipped on an icy flagstone, recovered and raced after him. But he only squealed, rolled down the incline toward the road, then gathered himself up and started back toward the porch. In my mind I ran with them, the three of us so weightless, so joyous our bare feet left no trace upon the fresh snow. Together Ellen and I circled after Mark, who was very pale and no longer laughing. His cough was so loud, such a terrible, breathless rattle I felt pain in my chest. Ellen was about to overtake him when he turned, lurched toward her and fell face down.

A steady amber light swept over them from the road as my father's Bronco followed the plough.

Ellen, holding Mark in her arms, screamed, "Carla, help."

My father must have heard her for he leapt out of

the Bronco and landed in a deep snow bank. At the same moment, Carla ran down the porch steps only to be slowed by the drift.

"Ellen, I'm coming," I shouted.

My father got to her first. By the time I reached the road he had pulled Carla and Mark into the car. Ellen was scrambling in after them.

"Wait," I yelled but my voice was lost in the roar of the motor as the Bronco sped away.

"Has the plough come through yet?" my mother asked over Lucy's TV squeals.

"Yes."

"Good. Your father will be home chilled to the bone anytime now."

I sat at the kitchen table while she prepared something in a bowl. Things moved before my eyes in slow motion. Butter plate, fork, napkin on a tray. A glass, a bottle of whiskey on the kitchen counter.

"There we are, all set," my mother was saying.

When I heard myself speak, things speeded up. Something fell in the sink with a metallic clatter. Bright light burst from the fridge and then went out.

"I think he's gone to the hospital."

Her mouth opened wide in a gasp.

"No, he's okay. It's Mark, Ellen's baby brother."

"What's the matter with him?" She came and sat beside me.

"He's sick. He went to sleep in Jesus's crib."

"What crib? Where?"

"Out in the cold." I began to cry and when she put her arm around me, I cried more.

My father came into the kitchen cursing the snow. He always had to be careful during the winter because the cold aggravated his sinus. Now he screwed up his face in pain. His trouser legs were soaked and clinging up to his knees.

"Is he going to be okay?" I asked through my tears.

"No."

"Oh dear. Are you sure?" My mother left me and went over to him.

"Sure, I'm sure. He'd stopped breathing." He poured himself a drink. "Poor little kid."

"Poor little thing," my mother said, momentarily disoriented, but then she recovered. "We ought to do something, maybe take some food over to the family. It's only eight o'clock and I have some lasagna in the freezer in case they're vegetarian or I could make…."

"Tomorrow," my father interrupted and went upstairs to get out of his wet clothes. His eyes were wet and not just from snow.

In the morning it snowed some more, a dry granulated snow that disappeared the instant the tiny grains touched the drifts, leaving Mark's small prints followed by Ellen's and Carla's clearly visible. And beyond the porch steps I could see a depression where the Holy Infant had lain half buried. St. Lucy's niche was empty. I had to concentrate very hard to visualize Mary and Joseph. The porch was empty. With Mark's death everyone had withdrawn.

At breakfast, my mother was uncertain if she should phone Mrs. Caswell before arriving with a hamper of food.

"She has always been very standoffish – very chilly."

My father agreed absentmindedly, though it was unclear to what.

"Maybe we should wait awhile," I suggested.

I longed to comfort Ellen, but I was not keen on my parents meeting the Caswells. My father had been wonderful in an effort to save Mark and my mother was trying to do the right thing with her hamper of food but neither of them knew anything about St. Lucy or the *nacimiento* and how it had been famous in the hot countries and why Mark had been in the crib. They hadn't seen Mary and Joseph.

At a meeting with Carla and Rolf, I could just hear my mother saying in her fond but unfocused way, "We do feel for you. Such a loss just at Christmas time."

If my father, not knowing what to say, told Rolf to be careful of the old tiles on the roof, I wouldn't be able to look Ellen in the eyes.

"There's no answer." My mother hung up the kitchen phone.

"I'll drive over around noon," my father said.

"We'll all go," my mother said.

I agreed, with misgivings.

The approach to the rear of the Caswell house was some distance away by means of an unused spur off an old county road well hidden by overgrown brush.

From the back seat I could see that my father was enjoying meeting the challenge of heavy drifts and buried ruts with his beloved Bronco. After crossing an open field, we entered a grove of white birches. Then, suddenly, the road curved and I saw up ahead a sort of courtyard formed by the rear wing of the house, a garage and a large shed, both built of the same rough-cut stone as the house. My father drove up to the back door and honked the horn. The sound, loud and harsh, exploded to create an airless silence around it. When there was no response I jumped out and going to the back door, looked through a glass pane into a large kitchen, empty except for an old fashioned range and a white enamel sink, badly chipped. Beyond the kitchen a dark hall led into a pantry. The open shelves were empty.

Since no one answered the doorbell I followed my father into the shed. It contained an ancient work bench and a woodstove.

"I guess they did whatever they did in here," he said, kicking a small pile of sawdust.

We went back outside. Against the shed wall, next to the door, were some stakes.

"Cheap stuff. The lumber yard practically gives it away. Not good for anything." He pointed to the knots. Caught on the splintered edge of one stake hung a torn piece of blue cotton cloth.

At the sight of it I heard Ellen saying, "The way they first came from Spain, just their heads and hands to be mounted on sticks covered by their costumes." My eyes blurred with tears.

"Where is everyone?" my mother asked. "The food will get cold." She got out of the car.

"Gone," my father answered, walking into the center of the courtyard. "Packed up and left." He pointed to wide tire tracks in the snow.

"Left how?"

"In an old converted school bus. I saw it when Caswell arrived at the hospital." He looked around the courtyard. "Strange people. Quiet enough but hard to figure. Guess you'll miss the girl. What was her name?"

"Ellen." Choking back the tears I explained that the Caswells had made something so beautiful out of nothing.

"Made what, where?" my mother asked.

"The *nacimiento*. Last night was St. Lucy's Feast. Mary and Joseph were there on the porch. Mark wanted to be Jesus."

They listened patiently, blinking their eyes from time to time as if that would help them understand.

"That's why he tried to sleep in the crib."

"Oh, I see," my mother said and my father nodded. But they couldn't possibly see when all I could show them was junk. Nevertheless, I went on talking. I had to get rid of the secrets that were weighing me down.

"We were friends, Ellen and I. I wanted us to be best friends. She told me lots of stories about the hot countries and I promised her snow for the *nacimiento* so that it would be like Bethlehem."

"I guess the children had never seen snow, poor things," Marge commented.

"Didn't know how to handle winter," Jake said.

For a moment the three of us stood stiff and silent, as if we were about to have our picture taken, each of us so comfortable, so ordinary in our moon boots and down-filled jackets with zippers, snaps, velcro fastenings, each of us clumsy in our concern: my mother, Marge, soap opera mom; my father, Dad, peace and quiet Jake already suffering from a cold after last evening's rescue effort. I saw my reflection in the Bronco's fender – skinny legs in stretch ski pants, big ear muffs, a muffler hanging down to my knees – dumb, top-heavy.

My father came over and handed me a kleenex. I wiped my eyes and got into the back seat next to the food hamper. No one spoke as we drove away. I couldn't speak. I had lost Ellen. I had given away all our secrets. I was as empty as that big, ugly house.

Up front, my mother slid over against my father. With his eyes fixed on the road, he put his right arm around her and drove one-handed, slowly but cool, like a guy out cruising.

It had stopped snowing. Pale sunlight transformed the grove of white birches enclosing us in a crystal web.

"I know what we'll do," my mother said. "We'll have a snow picnic in the pines behind our house."

She clapped her hands girlishly and smiled out the window. My father turned up the heater.

"Everything okay back there?" he asked.

"Yes, I'm all right."

When we reached our road I asked him to pull over beside the Caswell mailbox.

The leather of the hiking boots was frozen stiff and the skin of the oranges had shriveled. I stuffed the note to Ellen in my pocket and dropped the boots on the floor at my feet. In the enclosed heat of the car the oranges let out a sweet smell.

My mother turned to me and said, "I remember. St. Lucy puts oranges in the shoes of good children. I think that is so dear."

"Let's eat at home. My sinuses are killing me," my father said and pulled into our garage.

I was as glad as he was to get away from the snow.

The Geography Test 🍂

WHEN MISS HINTON pronounced "Krakatoa, Mt. St. Helens, Stromboli, or with a flourish pushed her blue tinted glasses into her orange-blonde hair and said "tectonic stress," the boy felt the tremors rise from the center of the earth and pass through the classroom floor into his bones. The knowledge that he lived on a fragile crust of a continent that floated on boiling rock and poisonous gases ever ready to explode and bury him like the child in the pictures of Pompeii trapped in the ashes of Vesuvius, Miss Hinton's favorite volcano, gave him nightmares. Nevertheless, geography was his favorite subject. In other classes he often stared at the globe and daydreamed himself back one hundred seventy million years when all the continents were united, South America and Africa, North America and Eurasia fitting neatly together like a jigsaw puzzle to form a single land mass. The world must have been one vast garden, a sort of Eden embraced by one ocean until fire and ice tore it all apart. Miss Hinton dealt fearlessly with eruptions and glaciers. The confidence with which she tapped the large hanging map of North America and took command of unstable ocean floors and drifting continents made him feel good.

Now, as she said, "Remember, class, we'll have a test tomorrow," he noticed a rugged face with blue eyes winking at him through the glass of the classroom door. He hadn't seen his father for a year and then the face had been flushed with anger.

When the bell rang, the map shuddered at Miss Hinton's touch and North America rolled up with a bang. The boy picked up his geography book and over the shuffle of feet heard a hoarse whisper, "Let's get the hell out of here."

A red pick-up was parked on the edge of the parking lot behind the school. As they walked to it, his father said, "When your Mom discovers you're gone, she'll let out a holler from here to Alaska."

The boy traced the holler's path west from Meedville across the Great Plains, over the Rockies and north to the Bering Straits, noting state boundaries and capitols on the way. The Pacific Northwest always gave him trouble. Oregon's borders blurred. He would have to study them before the test.

"She'll be mad as a snake," his father chuckled and unlocked the truck door.

"She sure will," the boy agreed, but only to make himself believe that he had a place, a secure niche in the drift of continents and that if he disappeared, someone might notice the vacancy and look for him. He didn't share his father's certainty that his mother would miss him immediately. His father hadn't been around to notice how tired and full of anger she was when she came home from waiting on tables at Bucky's Deluxe Diner, a job she had taken after his father had gone West.

"I'm beat. Here's supper, your favorite," she would say and hand him a plastic take-out container of Bucky's special of the day, spaghetti and meatballs or Salisbury steak, which he heated up while she sat at the kitchen table with a bottle of vodka.

Nights before his father's departure, he had overheard them arguing about leaving Meedville for Oregon. "Moving on" had been his father's phrase. The boy vaguely recalled having moved through a variety of elusive landscapes in the past: beaches littered with driftwood, deserts trembling with dust devils and silvery mirages. In contrast, Meedville was as solid as the brick buildings that lined the modest grid of streets laid out in the middle of farmland.

During a lesson on seismic regions, Miss Hinton had assured her students that although the continent was in constant motion, their particular spot on its crust was aseismic. Meedville was geologically dormant.

"It's a lousy backwater, no future, nothing's happening," his father had complained. The real action was in the forests of the Pacific Northwest. Lumber, paper products, construction were booming.

His mother had refused to move, saying she wasn't going to chase any more floating horse apples. Roots were important to her. The boy remembered a stay in a swampy place where the trees stood on tentacles in black water.

"He's gone," she had told him one morning at breakfast.

A deluge of postcards addressed to her arrived, first with pictures of wheat fields, then of oil rigs along with affectionate messages of love and kisses and requests for news. The boy deciphered the postmarks and followed the route on the map in his geography book. After several months, the cards depicted forests of enormous trees. The messages were angry. "*Not* missing you. I sure *don't* wish you were here."

His mother shrugged. "Like Hansel and Gretel, he's leaving a trail but I'm not chasing after him."

When the cards stopped, the boy worried but his mother said, "Never mind. He's probably moved into a gingerbread house."

True or not, his father was suddenly standing beside a red pick-up saying, "She'll more than holler. She'll phone Sheriff Jakes and scream 'Kidnapper, catch that kidnapper.'"

He mimicked her voice so perfectly that for an instant the boy believed it was happening. His father, having shouted like a maniac at Miss Hinton when she had questioned his parental authority to remove one of her students from school early, was now enjoying the prospect of "hitting the road and giving your Mom a jolt," but the scene had left the boy feeling helpless and he wasn't certain that being hunted by Sheriff Jakes was the greatest way of getting back home.

"Hop in." His father revved the motor.

He tossed his geography book onto the seat and climbed in. The plastic interior smelled new. "Where are we going?"

"You name it. We used to plan trips, just us two guys. Remember?"

The boy nodded. There had been many promises of camping in the Adirondacks, rafting down the Colorado, but now he wasn't interested. He had homework on his mind.

From the center of town, Main Street merged into a white concrete strip. Except for gas stations and fast food restaurants clustered at crossroads, the countryside was empty, the plowed fields streaked with snow. His father was talking about Southern California. The boy could see a blue ocean border along a pale yellow area of land veined with lines, the San Andreas fault, Miss Hinton's favorite example of earthquake country.

"We can live on the beach and pretend we're homeless," his father chuckled. "You think it over while I take care of some business in Hart's Motel ahead."

It was cold in the cab of the pick-up and without the keys he couldn't turn on the heater. He opened his book to study for the geography test, but the overhead light was dim and his eyes began to water from the strain. Hart's Motel was dark. However, on the roof above the entrance, a large neon heart pulsed on and off, changing from pink to darker red. Beneath it, steady blue letters spelled "Vacancy." Now the highway was a bright stream of headlights as people drove home from work.

His mother would be sitting at the kitchen table, but not missing him yet. Some days, when he had Junior Chess Club, or band practice, he didn't get home until six. Today he had neither, but she probably wouldn't think to look at the schedule of his activities he had taped on the refrigerator door for her.

His father emerged from the darkness of the motel office and slid behind the wheel. As they pulled away, the boy glanced in the side mirror to see a young woman in the driveway. She was waving, drowning in deeper and deeper crimson.

"Where to?" his father asked as they merged into the highway traffic.

"Let's visit Grandma," he answered, suddenly remembering that she lived on a farm just outside of Meedville.

"Sorry, pal, no can do. Grandma's dead. Your Mom didn't tell you?"

"Maybe she doesn't know."

"Yeah, or maybe she just forgot."

"I'm kind of hungry," the boy lied, stalling for time. To his surprise, his father didn't seem in any hurry. Maybe they were going to play hide and seek with the sheriff on the edge of town and "get her attention but good" before really taking off.

Sirens, distant but coming rapidly closer, sounded over the whir of traffic.

"Hang on. Jakes and his posse are after us." His father leaned on the horn and passing several cars at high speed, turned off the highway onto a dark secondary road.

The tires whined as they hit the asphalt that curved

sharply and continued to wind through a wooded area. In the mirror on his side, the boy glimpsed powerful headlights and a red flasher that at each twist in the road leaped out and then back into the woods. As the pick-up gained speed, the lights and siren were left behind in the tree dense darkness.

"We've shaken them," his father sighed after the road swerved into flat open country.

The boy caught his breath and slumped against the car door.

Suddenly a blaze of red and white light flooded through the back window. His father stepped on the accelerator. The pick-up lurched forward but was passed instantly by a white vehicle with sirens blaring.

"Go to hell," his father yelled out the window at the ambulance and slowed to the side of the road. "You still hungry?"

"Sort of."

"Okay, we'll eat. I know a terrific steak place."

They drove back onto the highway and headed toward Meedville.

The steak place, a cinnamon brown building with white wrought-iron grills on the windows, was crowded. Men in blue and yellow satin jackets with bowling team names stitched on the back crowded around the bar.

"Hi, guys." A large man came from behind the bar and punched his father on the shoulder.

His father laughed and grabbed the man's arm. "Harry, you old s.o.b. This is my son. He's starving and I'm bone dry."

"Sit in that booth over there, Sonny. Thelma will bring you our super special while I take care of your old man," Harry said.

It was the biggest burger he had ever seen, a triple decker that oozed juices and mustard when he poked it with a fork. He was too tired to eat, too tired to think about the state capitals and Oregon's boundaries that were sure to be on Miss Hinton's test. At the end of the bar his father, standing apart from the milling crowd of bowlers, was making rings on the counter with his wet glass. His face was angry and with each ring his lips moved. The boy read the "F" word.

The front door opened and the sturdy figure of Sheriff Jakes, followed by a deputy, went over and stood behind his father. His father must have sensed something for he raised his eyes to catch the reflections in the bar mirror. Then he smiled and turning around held out his hand.

"Hi, Rob. How's the fella? I guess the wife called you to find me and the boy."

Jakes ignored the outstretched hand. "Cut the crap, Sam. Carol didn't call me, but Winter's Ford agency did, to report that red pick-up you took from their lot as stolen."

The bowlers shoved their hands in the pockets of their shiny jackets and stood suddenly silent as if at a tournament. Harry leaned across the bar and whispered something to his father who nodded and handed the car keys to the sheriff. As they walked toward the door, his father called, "Tell your Mom to pay more attention next time. Tell her…." The words were swept away in a draft of cold air.

"Com' on, son, I'll drive you home," the deputy said.

The kitchen lights were on when they arrived at the house.

"You okay?" the deputy asked.

"Sure. My Mom's home. She's waiting for me."

"Don't forget your book."

His mother, seated at the table, smiled and pointed to the white plastic container. "Your favorite, eggplant parmesan. Pineapple cheesecake in the fridge."

"Thanks, I've eaten." He sat down opposite her.

"Oh." She tilted her head to one side and giggled. "We'll feed it to the raccoons."

"I'll make us some coffee and then I've got to study for a geography test."

"Geography test?" She stared at the map of the u.s. on the jacket of his book.

"Yeah, for Miss Hinton's class. We have to be able to identify mountain ranges, rivers, forests, stuff like that." He placed two mugs on the table and removed the bottle and glass.

"Forests, Oregon has forests."

"So does Brazil," he said, sensing danger.

She ran an unsteady finger up the Pacific coast. "I never believed in Oregon. Oh, it's on the map but I wouldn't go there." Her finger slid off California into the ocean. "We belong here." She leaned over and pressed her face close to the book. "Meedville's not on the map. Nobody would be able to find it. We'd disappear and nobody would miss us."

47

He got up and stood beside her as she sobbed out of control.

There was a knock at the door. The round face of Pete Harris, Meedville's only policeman, looked through the glass. The boy waved him in.

"What's happened? Something terrible has happened," his mother screamed.

"Don't upset yourself, Ma'am. Miss Hinton called about some trouble at the school. The principal reported your boy missing."

"My boy's here," she cried, and grabbed his belt. "We're going to have supper. I would have missed him."

"Sure you would." Harris backed out the door.

He kept the bedside light lit and lying face down, grasped the sides of the mattress. The tremors were slight and although the drift was slow, deep beneath the surface a fiery chaos threatened. Miss Hinton whipped off her blue tinted glasses and said, "Do not be afraid. Meedville is not earthquake country," and with a flick of her finger she spun the globe. The continents flowed back together, the ocean breathed in gentle regular tides and he slept.

The Little Girls and Their Dolls ⌀

THE LITTLE GIRLS dress their little girl dolls in black; black velvet, taffeta, moiré.

"What, no blue to match eyes, no rosy pink to compliment cheeks?" the mothers ask. They have made doll gowns from pink and blue remnants of their girlhood party dresses.

"Black is best," the little girls say.

The little girls' Grannies, their mothers' mothers, shrink daily until they are as small as the girls. Some wander away from home, are found and put elsewhere. Others vanish. Mothers go looking.

Dolls' mothers' mothers are found in attics. Their bright silks are still bright but their cheeks are powdered gray with dust. A limb or two are missing.

At the sight the little girls and their dolls cry and dig burial holes in the dark.

"What, no moonlight, no starlight?" the mothers ask.

"Dark is best," the little girls answer and wrap themselves in their shadows.

Mothers plead, "Leave your bed time toys, those nightmare dolls. Come play in the daylight."

"Night lasts," the little girls whisper amongst themselves.

"Why do you all leave me alone while you play Hide and Seek?" fathers call out angrily.

"It's not a game," the little girls reply and hide with their dolls under the stairs.

Last Holes ✍

"H1, A L," she says and tells him to call her Gloria.

He has never seen her in his bar before and she is friendly, real friendly like a stray which makes him wary. However, she is his first customer of the evening so he says "hi" and watches while she arranges herself on the bar stool, then rummages in her handbag. A lipstick and cigarette lighter spill out onto the bar followed by a key chain entangled in a pair of sun glasses.

"If you're out of cigarettes, there's a machine by the door."

"Those machines never have my brand. Anyway here they are." She places a pack of Benson and Hedges on the bar and scoops the other items back into the purse. "I'll have a double Chivas Regal, no water. If you haven't got Chivas…."

"I have it."

At five dollars a shot his regular neighborhood customers aren't ordering Chivas Regal these days, not with all the layoffs, but as a matter of pride he keeps a bottle. Before locating it in back of the cheap blends, he takes his time to check her out in the mirror behind the bar.

Pale blonde, early forties, nice tan, no jewelry except for a wedding ring set with diamonds. She wears the mink like it was an old sweater wrapped around her shoulders. The mist in her blue eyes tells him this isn't her first drink of the evening. As he reaches for the bottle, she meets his eyes in the reflection, smiles and puts a twenty dollar bill on the bar.

"Just rocks, no water," she says. "Got the place pretty much to myself. Well, the night is young as they say." She looks at the round clock with the green neon sign "Al's Place" over the front door. "You had this place long?"

He concentrates on the thin stream of whiskey flowing over the ice. She needs to talk, to tell her story. He recognizes the symptoms: the tension in the voice, the tight grip on the glass.

"Since I came back from Nam," he says and opens the tap in the sink. An old trick. He has heard too many stories but doesn't like to hurt anyone's feelings by seeming uninterested. The sound of the running water helps filter out the monotonous repetition of "I, me, I, I." Gloria is a surprise. She isn't talking about herself but about golf, how she and her husband always played together. It seems she loves the game. She pauses from time to time to order another drink and ask, "You understand?"

He nods and watches the water curl around the drain. It streams into a small irregular pond surrounded by grass. A difficult approach shot to the green. The three and five iron are his best clubs. Any hacker can wallop the ball off the tee but afterwards precision, control count.

The body stretches, finds its rhythm, pivots and lets the club head follow through. At contact, a crisp snap of metal, the ball lifts in a trajectory from grass to sky, arcs beyond the hazards of water and sand and drops. The green, fast, smooth as a fine pelt, would shed it but back spin counters the momentum. The ball stops dead sixteen inches from the hole.

"Another of the same, Al." Gloria rolls the empty glass between her palms and smiles boozily at new faces in the mirror.

He pours one ounce over rocks. She has found a wider audience and may not notice. The bar is filling up with his regular customers. He hurries to serve them. Now his place feels good. The crowd is congenial, the hour warm in the green light of "Al's Place". He moves along the bar passing steins of beer into the outstretched hands.

"How about me and make it an honest double."

Gloria's voice breaks above the subdued hum. A couple of the men look her over and move away.

"Lady, you've had enough. Time to go home." He hits the cash register and hands her the check. He wants her out, gone before she spoils the good feeling. His regulars, guys laid off the graveyard shift when the mill cut back, need a quiet beer and no women around, especially a non-stop talker from the other side of town.

She pays the check but makes no move to leave.

"Listen, Al. Charlie putted for par on the eighth. It was beautiful and then...."

She chokes up, looks around for someone to share her widow's woes and applaud Charlie's last feat.

Joe Carr down the line mutters, "The poor bastard dropped dead at the country club and left her all his dough. Right, Al?"

"She's leaving, Joe."

Carr, out of work with six kids, is hurting. Al removes her glass. "I'll call a cab, okay?"

She doesn't answer. She's off on something new and leans toward Hank Rowley and his brother Tom who stare as if they were watching some TV talking head. It's not golf talk. It's Jesus. This evening she found Jesus in Al's parking lot. He was seated on the bumper of her car, Charlie's old Jag.

"I told Jesus how Charlie and I meant everything to each other. Now Charlie's gone. I'm alone. Jesus understood."

"Like the bumper sticker says, Gloria, 'Jesus saves'," Rowley laughs and licks the beer foam off his upper lip.

"Wrong. Jesus loves," Gloria flares, then sags against the bar.

Al helps her to the cab. Now she's gone he can relax with the regulars who nurse their beers and argue cars and sports.

"Hey, Al. You're a golfer," Rowley says.

"Was until a piece of shrapnel connected with my shoulder and destroyed my swing. As a kid I caddied at the country club and Bill Thomas, the pro, used to let me play the course after hours."

"Then you know the hole where Charlie had his heart attack."

"The eighth. A par four."

"Gloria sure wanted to talk about it and what a great golfer Charlie was. How come you froze her out?"

"I didn't want to spoil her story. The fact is I used to birdie the eighth."

"What the hell does that mean? You're the only golfer here."

"I made it in three, one under par."

"So you were damned good."

He admits to a low handicap.

Rowley turns on his stool and calls into the crowd, "Hey, guys, listen to this."

"Lay off, Hank. It's closing time. Everybody drink up."

He follows the men out to get a breath of air and unwind before locking up. The streets are dark and deserted, some of the stores have been burned out, others are boarded up, but his parking lot is brightly lit by floodlights. A few of the men hang around and continue to argue football scores. Out of work, they are in no hurry to go home. The parking lot empties gradually. Alone near the entrance the Jag gleams under the lights. He walks over to it. The car is unlocked, keys left on the dash. On the back seat two golf bags lie side by side. Cute, real cute, just like a pair of lovers. The trunk is full of stuff, a large umbrella, wind breakers, a bucket of practice balls, a couple of them red for playing in snow. Crazy but great with only a few fanatics on the course. The woman's bag fits in the trunk but there is no room for the man's, a lightweight burgundy nylon with blue vinyl trim, unlike those leather monsters he carried as a caddy, so heavy the strap cut into his shoulder. Charlie was a big man to judge by the length of the steel shafts of the clubs. He has never seen such a lot of clubs in one man's bag. The woods with their blue and red needle point covers, Gloria's handiwork no doubt, number one through five. Okay, some players favor the woods but all these irons, he counts twenty, not even the pros carry more than twelve.

"Some machine, Al." Rowley strokes one sleek burgundy fender and looks inside to inspect the interior. "Mahogany veneer, dark red leather upholstery, the real thing."

"And she leaves it unlocked with two beautiful sets of clubs. She's lucky the car is still here."

Rowley climbs into his '76 Ford pick-up and calls out the window, "Jesus understands. He loves drunks."

The truck disappears into the darkness leaving the parking lot empty. He calculates that from where he is standing a seven iron should make it to the open door of his place. Charlie's club is too long for him and a slight slope of the asphalt causes the ball to roll behind his left foot until it meets a dead leaf and stops. Not a bad lie but if he hooks the ball will end up on Euclid Avenue. A slice will send it into the Gulf station on First Street. As he takes a practice half-swing the muscles in his shoulder seize up. Down the fairway green light glows in the open doorway. He shortens his grip, addresses the ball and swings, firm follow through, no back spin. The ball lifts, carries straight to the landing and runs on into the bar. A hole in one. Terrific. Lucky.

Pathetic. Pain radiates down his left arm and blurs his vision. He picks up the bag and walks across the lot. The bag with all the extra irons is heavy. Big Charlie must have been a lousy golfer, always hoping some magic club would do the job for him, a real duffer who got a lucky par on the eighth, but never made it to the ninth tee.

Inside his place he retrieves the ball from under a bar stool. The ninth, a trappy dog-leg to the left. Always was a bad hole for him. Every player has one, a repeated disaster to be analyzed over and over. Maybe he used to tense up, hands got ahead of the club head, left arm bent. Anyway, he blew it time and again. His best score was a bogey. The memory sticks like a burr. When Gloria comes for the Jag and Charlie's clubs, he'll tell her about it. She'll understand what he's talking about, even if she's high on Scotch and Jesus. She'll understand.

Best of Friends ℘

MIKEY AND FRANK, Rita and Gina were best friends and had been ever since they were little kids growing up within a radius of ten city blocks. In their last year in high school Mikey and Rita, Frank and Gina became lovers.

That spring after graduation the boys got jobs in Frank's uncle's body shop. At noon they sat behind the shop in Frank's old Pontiac convertible, ate lunch and said, "Rita and Gina, they're terrific. Rita's fantastic. Gina's beautiful." They spoke in choppy phrases as if out of breath.

Rita and Gina met on their breaks in the employees' lounge of Hart's department store. Rita was in notions, Gina in lingerie. Their voices were soft as if each were talking to herself about love.

Saturday evenings the four of them gathered, usually at Rita's place. They all lived with their parents but Rita's mother was dead and her father always went bowling so they could sit in the apartment living room and discuss what they were going to do. Mikey and

Frank, wary of being bossed, kept the initiative by agreeing ahead of time on where to go and what to do even if it was only to walk down the block for a pizza. Rita and Gina accepted the plan but not without vigorous arguments and alternative suggestions until Mikey who was short-tempered exploded and threatened that he and Frank would go out on their own. By the end of the evening they split into couples, each going a separate way to make love.

In May Rita's birthday fell on a Saturday. Mikey had given a lot of thought to the arrangements and a week prior to the date he announced that they would begin the day by taking the subway from Queens to Manhattan. The girls were to wear dresses, no slacks, summer dresses and straw hats. Rita with her long dark hair and pale face would look terrific in a straw hat. They would go rowing on the lake in Central Park. He and Frank would do the rowing. Sure they knew how. "Easy," they declared and squatting side by side on the gritty stoop of the walk-up where Frank lived they maneuvered oars and grunted in unison. They'd rowed lots of times.

"With lots of girls," Gina whispered to Rita and the girls laughed quietly with their heads together because while there had been lots of girls and lots of boys in the past now there were just the four of them.

"It's a great idea, Mikey," Rita said but the next day during the coffee break she confessed to Gina that the thought of the lake, of being on water terrified her. She had never been in a row boat or any other kind of boat. She didn't know how to swim, none of them did.

"Frank and Mikey say the lake is real shallow," Gina reported.

"Those two say a lot of things," Rita replied and on Saturday morning as the four of them entered the park and walked toward the boat shed she left Mikey's side and linked arms with Gina.

The boys hurried on ahead.

After a few steps Rita needed to rest for a minute. She and Gina left the path for the shade of some trees at the edge of the lake. The air was too humid to feel fresh but the spring green branches cut the glare of the sun. Gina went to sit on the grass, then remembered her new dress and leaned against a tree trunk.

"Have you told Mikey?" she asked facing Rita.

"Not yet. Maybe tonight I'll tell him." Rita fanned her face with her hat.

"Mikey likes kids. He's been teaching my sister's little boy to box."

"And if it's a girl?"

"He could teach her how to row," Gina laughed.

"Maybe I'll tell him after we get out of the boat and are back on land."

Rita peered through the trees at the lake. In the center a cluster of boats zigged and zagged erratically over the muddy water while the occupants hooted at the inept oarsmen. A few boats swept smoothly past the crowd and disappeared behind a rocky promontory.

"We ought to go. Mikey's already pissed about our keeping them waiting," Gina said.

"In a minute. Look there, just beyond where those branches almost touch the water."

"I don't see anything. Some shadows, a bunch of weeds."

"Okay. It's in those tall weeds."

Rita's hand trembled as she pointed to a small naked body snared in a clump of reeds and floating face down, the bulges of the little head and buttocks just visible above the surface of the water.

Mikey and Frank were already in the boat when the girls, gasping and wide eyed, ran onto the pier.

"Shut up and get in," Mikey yelled and shoved the oars into the water.

Frank helped them into the stern and then pushed the boat away from the pier. He and Mikey rowed in short choppy strokes so that the oar just skimmed the water and the boat hardly moved.

"Over there. Hurry. Go over there," Rita screamed and stood up.

The boat tilted, Frank's oar coming out of the water completely while Mikey's sent the boat spinning in a half circle.

"Grab her before she sinks us," Frank called.

Gina pulled Rita back down beside her.

"Mikey, do something. There's a baby in the water over there," Rita sobbed and pressed her face against Gina's shoulder.

Mikey nodded to Frank and after a few strokes drew in the oars and let the boat drift while they scanned the shore. Something half-hidden bobbed in the murky water and then disappeared in a tangle of weeds and tree roots.

"We're getting out of here," Mikey said through clenched teeth and drawing hard on his oar turned the boat around.

"There comes a cop," Gina cried.

She and Rita waved their hats but the policeman patrolling the path on a motor scooter was intent on avoiding pedestrians. The trees that fringed the shore line soon hid him from view.

Mikey and Frank, sweating through their t-shirts, rowed into the crowded center of the lake. A dull thud shook the boat as it sideswiped another heavily loaded with Orientals of all ages. Small children howled in terror. Male adults shouted in a foreign language and raised their fists.

"Sorry," Mike called back and then muttered, "Fucking Albanians."

Frank laughed. Mikey called everyone outside their neighborhood "Albanian."

"More like fucking boat people," Frank said.

"You guys aren't funny," Gina snapped.

"I'm going to be sick," Rita gasped and leaned over the side of the boat.

Gina grabbed her at the waist.

"Sick. Get this, Frank. First she sees a dead baby. Now she's seasick in a pond." Mikey glared, his broad face flushed with anger.

"Take us back to land," Gina said quietly but so fiercely Mikey blinked as if she had slapped him.

He looked at his watch. "I paid for an hour. I've still got twenty minutes."

"Leave us off. We'll wait for you on land. I need to get out of the sun," Rita pleaded.

"We'll all stay together," Mikey said and he and Frank rowed toward the pier.

On a knoll shaded by a young copper beech Gina sat on the grass. Nearby Rita lay curled on her side, her hat over her face as if to shut out the voices of Mikey and Frank who were commenting on the girls who walked by on the path below. A sudden scream, steady and piercing as a siren, silenced the boys and brought Rita and Gina to their feet. Directly below them a young woman struggled with a little girl who squatted on the path and refused to budge.

"Swim, swim," the child shrieked.

"She can't swim," the young woman said and picked up the doll that had fallen from the child's hands onto the pavement. Its naked body was wet and streaked with mud.

"There's your drowned baby," Mikey nudged Rita.

In the woman's arms the doll rolled back its eyelids and stared up at them with glittering blue eyes.

"It sure looks lifelike," Frank said in a subdued voice. He reached for Gina's hand.

"Yeah, lifelike and dead in the water," Mikey answered.

"You guys are really sick," Rita, pale and shaky, drew away from them.

When Mikey reached out to prevent her from backing down the slope, she ran past him onto the path and into the crowd.

"I'm leaving tomorrow morning. Aunt Ethel is always glad to have me," Rita told Gina on the phone that evening.

Gina had visited Rita's Aunt Ethel while they were still in high school and she remembered a large energetic woman with bleached hair and sad eyes who had been going steady for years with Henry Henderson, proprietor of Henderson and Son Memorial Chapel Mortuary and Complete Services, founded by his grandfather. Aunt Ethel carried with her an aroma of nail polish, perm and other chemical odors from the beauty parlor she ran in the basement of an imposing but decrepit Victorian mansion. Upstairs the turreted red brick fortress had been converted into modest apartments. Aunt Ethel's spare room was in the tower section. Rita planned to stay there.

"What about Mikey, the baby?" Gina asked.

"I can't talk to Mikey now. We both need time to get our heads together. Promise you won't tell where I am."

Gina promised and went to bed. It had been a rotten day for everyone. Mikey had tried so hard to impress Rita. After her sudden departure that had left him bewildered and furious, he had declared that Gina and Frank should visit the park zoo with him.

"Let's go see the rest of the monkeys," he had snarled.

Gina hated watching caged animals and Frank knew it. She had expected him to suggest something else but he had whispered, "Come on. Mikey's hurting. He needs us," and then he had followed Mikey into the monkey house leaving her to wait outside on a park bench.

Early the next morning, Sunday, the phone woke Gina.

"Where the hell is Rita?" Mikey yelled.

When he refused to believe that she didn't know she hung up.

At noon Frank called to say he wanted to see her. He was coming over.

"Don't," she said and hung up.

He came anyway and parked the Pontiac with the top down in front of the building.

Her mother noticed the car from the kitchen window and asked, "You and Frank having problems?"

"Yes, and Rita and Mikey, too."

"You'll make up. You're all such good friends," her mother said and waved out the window.

Frank took the wave as an invitation and when he arrived breathless from having raced up the stairs three at a time Gina agreed to go to the beach.

"What's with you and Rita? Mikey's going crazy," he said the minute she got in the car.

"Just keep your eyes on the road and both hands on the wheel." She removed his arm from around her shoulder.

"Okay, okay. I won't touch." He let his arm fall between them but continued to drive with one hand. "Where is Rita? Mikey's beating his head in trying to figure out why she acted so weird in the park."

Gina turned on the radio and her "Rita can't swim

and you guys can't row" was lost in the rush of sea air and baseball scores that swirled around the open car.

In the hot sticky weeks that followed the thought of Rita and the baby weighed more and more heavily on Gina, especially because she was seeing more of Mikey than she ever had before. He was lonely and on the evenings during the week when she and Frank sat in the Pontiac outside her place – parked to save money on gas – Mikey always showed up with a six pack.

"Any news from the missing person?" he would ask and slide in next to Gina.

After she shook her head he would lean across her and challenge Frank about some baseball player's average. For the rest of the evening they argued sports as if she weren't there.

On the weekends when she went out with Frank alone she sensed some of Mikey's anger growing in him. One rainy afternoon they drove to the South Shore and parked facing the deserted beach. The rain drummed gently on the canvas roof and enclosed the car in its own soft sound. Gina moved closer to Frank but he leaned forward to hug the steering wheel and stare at the ocean.

"Dumb, real dumb," he muttered and counted each wave as it hurtled against the breakwater and snaked in gray green coils between the rocks before disintegrating in puddles on the sand.

When he got to wave twelve Gina interrupted him. "The ocean isn't dumb. It just is," she said and touched his arm.

66

He turned on her. "You and Rita have been bullshitting Mikey and me for months."

"And you and Mikey have been hassling me for months. Let's talk about something else."

He leaned back beside her. "Okay, about that time in the park."

"That's not something else."

Arguing turned him on but now when he went to kiss her he was like a blind man running his fingers over her face, groping frantically for her mouth with his lips. She stiffened in his arms and kept her eyes fixed on his. He released his hold.

"What's the matter, babe? You got a case of frigidity all of a sudden?"

"I'm scared," she sobbed against his chest.

"Scared, what the hell of?"

"Maybe Mikey and Rita don't really love each other."

"And you're really nuts. Mikey hasn't even looked at another girl since Rita left and a sexy guy like him has had plenty of chances with those dolls in and out of the body shop with their Mercedes. I'll bet Rita, wherever she is, is fu...."

"Don't say it. Don't you and Mikey even think that." She pulled away from him.

"Shit." He counted a last wave through the rain-streaked windshield and then turned the key in the ignition.

"Wait, Frank. We've got to talk before things get any more screwed up between you and me. Mikey and Rita have problems. They're our friends but they're giving us problems."

He turned off the motor and looked at her sullenly.

"Rita's in Albany with Aunt Ethel. She's going to have a baby, Mikey's baby, but she doesn't want him to know until after it's born in October."

"Why not? Ever since that day in the park I figured she was a flake." He choked in anger repeating, "It's his baby. He has a right to know," and pounded a fist into the palm of his free hand as if to fight his way out of the tangle of his thoughts.

Finally she convinced him to stop cursing and to listen. "I'll go to Albany this coming weekend. Aunt Ethel says Rita is feeling lousy. I'll cheer her up and convince her to tell Mikey now."

On the drive home Frank promised to keep the baby a secret. "But I don't feel good about it. Mikey's my best friend."

"And Rita's mine," Gina said.

As Gina approached the red brick mansion she noticed a new sign next to the basement door. *Ethel's Beauty Salon Styling Perms Tints Frosts Hair Weaving.* Apparently Aunt Ethel had expanded her services although it seemed unlikely that her staid elderly ladies would use them. Aunt Ethel, tinted and frosted, met her outside the door with a hug. Her gray eyes were tired under the blue eye shadow and mascara. Gina followed her past the dryers where three drowsy faces, rosy cheeked from the heat, looked like painted eggs.

"You can leave your bag in here," Aunt Ethel said leading the way into an empty booth. She drew the plastic curtain behind her and grabbing some wet towels off the chair in front of the basin motioned to Gina to sit down.

"Nothing more disgusting than a messy salon but what with worries about Rita and the baby and my regular ladies needing me, I can't keep up." She drew a stool next to a manicurist's table and sat down, resting her arms on the pillow. "The baby, a girl, arrived night before last, no, I guess it was the night before that. Anyway a very premature little thing. Rita wants you to see it right away. She's at the hospital now."

"Is she okay?"

"She's been released from the hospital but we worry about the baby." Aunt Ethel began to fidget with the bottles of nail polish. "I'd come with you but when I finish here I have to go over to Mr. Henderson's. Emily Watkins, one of my regulars, passed away and needs doing. Her pin curls take forever and the viewing and rosary are this evening."

Gina recalled that the relationship between Aunt Ethel and Henry Henderson had professional as well as sentimental dimensions. When family and friends of the deceased filed in front of the open coffin they always noticed the hair first and would whisper, "Ethel does it exactly right, just so life-like."

"Ethel, I'm ready for a comb out and Henry's here for you," one of the egg faces called from under the dryer.

Aunt Ethel jumped up and opened the plastic curtain. Gina found herself facing a tall thin man in a dark suit. At Aunt Ethel's suggestion he agreed to run Gina over to the hospital three blocks down the street while Aunt Ethel did the comb out. On his return she would be ready to work on Emily Watkins at his funeral home.

Mr. Henderson escorted Gina to a black stretch limo and opened the door opposite the driver's seat. Inside it smelled faintly of pine scented air freshener and outside on each of the front fenders a chrome standard supported a furled purple and white funeral flag.

"I drove Rita to the hospital, no time to call for an ambulance. I thought I might have to deliver the baby," Mr. Henderson said as he got behind the wheel.

"Have you seen the baby?"

"Just once when I took Ethel over. They're quite strict about visitors' viewing hours but you'll get in." He tapped the digital clock in the panelled dashboard.

The limo purred at a red light.

"I hope the baby will be okay," Gina sighed.

"Hard to know. Three and one half pounds, two and a half months premature." He took one black gloved hand off the steering wheel and rested it palm up in the air as if to weigh the infant. "Not much to work with."

"How do you mean 'work with'?" Gina gasped.

"Here we are," he said stopping in front of the hospital, an ugly brick building similar to those that lined the block. "The nursery is on the third floor."

Gina found herself in a group of elated grandparents and young fathers crowding around windows along one side of a nursery where the infants could be seen in cribs arranged in three rows. A masked nurse walked from one crib to another and apparently by pre-arrangement lifted a baby up for the family to see.

"The preemies are down the hall," a young woman in the pink smock of a volunteer told Gina.

At a single window a small subdued gathering stared into a brightly lit room. The infants in the front row incubators were visible but those behind them were difficult to see. At the back of the room Rita, masked and gowned, reached one hand through an opening in the incubator's side. With two fingers she was gently massaging a tiny area of pink flesh, the rest of the body was enmeshed in a web of tubes and wires. Gina could just make out a tiny head covered with a film of dark hair and one scrawny leg bent inward at the knee. On the wall above Rita's head greenish lines and numbers flashed across a screen.

A voice on a loud speaker announced the end of visiting hours and it was only then that Rita looked up and saw Gina waving to her.

As they walked the three blocks back to Aunt Ethel's, Rita talked without stopping. The baby, she called her baby Gina, was doing well. Soon all the support systems could be removed. Of course, her lungs were under developed, her heart weak. The doctors were cautious. The infant's condition varied from hour to hour. Gina waited to hear Mikey's name. When Rita didn't mention him she asked "Who does the baby look like?"

"Not like me. She has blue eyes," Rita replied and stretched out on Aunt Ethel's living room sofa. "I'm so tired, just like the baby."

Gina sat beside her. She looked pale but she was well groomed, her once long dark hair had been well cut and her nails manicured – Aunt Ethel's work. While Rita dozed Gina bided her time composing different ways of saying "you must send for Mikey" and letting her eyes wander around the room. A few straight backed chairs stood aligned so symmetrically along a wall they could've been nailed to the floor. One tall unshuttered window of clear plate glass admitted a northern light that combined with the sparse furnishing to suggest the anonymity of a waiting room, an antechamber beyond whose walls some private activity was taking place. A large fireplace with a massive grey marble mantel stood boarded over at one end of the room, a reminder of the days when the entire apartment was part of a vast reception hall. On either side of the fireplace walls were covered with photographs of Aunt Ethel's regular ladies. They gazed calmly into space, their grey hair in tight pin curls or swept and lacquered in bouffant piles. Gina got up and went over to read the handwritten expressions of affection and dates going back thirty-five years.

"The special ones are over the fireplace," Rita said in a drowsy voice.

The special ones were lined up in free-standing frames on the mantelpiece. Gina stood on tiptoe to scrutinize them. Gradually the images came into focus: doll-like features so fixed they appeared to be overlaid with gesso, figures, young and old, recumbent on white satin, their cheeks blushed with rouge, their crimson lips smiling faintly. One special one, a little girl with Shirley Temple curls, had been treated with a lighter touch and as a result looked sweetly life-like in her small coffin. The silver frame was unique as well, heart shaped with the child at the center surrounded by smaller photos of what Gina took to be parents, grandparents, and a tank of tropical fish.

"Those on the mantel are Aunt Ethel's special friends. She did them for free," Rita murmured and stared at the heart shaped frame. Then sobbing she pulled the blanket over her face.

"I'm calling Frank to tell Mikey he's a father," Gina said and went into the kitchen.

The din of the body shop made communication difficult but finally she got her message across and heard him yell, "Hold on while I tell Mikey." A roar of male voices and machinery followed and then Mikey came on shouting, "We're coming. Frank and I'll be there tomorrow."

"Can't see a goddamn thing," Mikey strained against the glass of the nursery window.

He was still smarting from his run-in with the head nurse who at his demand that he be allowed inside had been told only parents were permitted. Also he should please keep his voice down and stand outside with the other visitors. To make matters worse, he had decided in his excitement that his baby was one in the front row, a rosy infant.

When Gina identified the incubator for him he

snarled, "Nothing but tubes and wires," to Frank who nodded and hunched deeper into his leather jacket.

At Gina's insistence they had come directly to the hospital. She had wanted Mikey to see the baby before going to Aunt Ethel's where Rita after a bad night of bleeding and nightmares was still in bed. They had arrived tired and dirty. The Pontiac had broken down along the way. Both had worked under it.

"She is still very small but you can see her vital signs on that screen," Gina said as Mikey, cursing under his breath and rocking back and forth on his heels, disturbed the people behind him.

"Go get Rita." Frank held out the car keys.

"I'll walk," Mikey said and headed down the hall to the elevators.

Frank wanted to follow, to get the hell out. The place gave him the creeps. Besides, he was hungry. Gina agreed to go with him to a deli across the street where he had to eat his pastrami on rye standing up while she watched the hospital entrance in case Rita arrived.

"Mikey freaked out when he heard about the kid. Then he was pissed at Rita for not telling him that she was pregnant; but once we got on the thruway he was okay," Frank said. He blew on the steaming coffee and then added, "We didn't expect it to look like that."

"Like what?"

"Like drowned. Half dead. I mean, it's weird lying there hooked up to a TV so all you can see is some lumps." He gulped down the coffee and absently crushed the empty container in one hand.

Gina took it from him and placed it in a wastebasket.

"You and Mikey expected Mother Mary and baby Jesus," she said.

"Don't lay that crap on us. On the phone you told me it's a preemie and that it looks like Mikey so that's what I told him. 'Preemie' sounds cute, right? Maybe it'll look better tomorrow."

"It is not it. It's she and no she won't, not for a while."

Gina stepped out the door and crossed the street to the hospital. When she arrived at the window the only people inside the nursery were a doctor and a couple of nurses. They blocked her view of baby Gina's incubator. She looked at the monitor on the wall. The screen was blank.

"Gina, come."

She followed the bleached hair through the gathering of visitors into a small waiting room across the hall. An elderly couple sat silently beside a rubber plant in one corner of the room.

"Come sit down here," Aunt Ethel said and handed Gina a kleenex.

"Does Rita know?"

"Yes. She phoned me right after the hospital called her. I rushed upstairs. The wet heads and comb outs will manage without me for once."

"How's she taking it?"

"Hard, very hard. No tears. As soon as you get yourself together you must go to her." Aunt Ethel pulled another kleenex out of her shoulder bag and blew her nose. "Her boyfriend is with her and as I was about to come here his friend arrived."

"Mikey and Frank. They're friends."

Aunt Ethel nodded and left her chair to look up and down the corridor. A nurse with bobbed black hair stopped, patted her hand and hurried on.

"One of my regulars," Aunt Ethel said returning to her seat. "Yes, Mikey and Frank are with Rita. I explained to Mikey that arrangements have to be made."

"Arrangements?"

"First of all there's the death certificate, I'm waiting for the doctor to sign it. Otherwise the hospital morgue won't release the body. There's Mr. Henderson now." She gave Gina a quick hug and hurried after him.

The living room was empty but Gina could hear Mikey and Rita talking in the bedroom, Rita's voice calm, Mikey's choked. She went into the kitchen to make some coffee and found Frank putting a six pack in the refrigerator.

"They're talking. That's good," Gina said.

"They weren't talking just a while ago. Maybe they were doing something better."

She turned away from him and plugged in the percolator.

"Now all Rita can talk about is the fucking funeral," Mikey said coming into the kitchen. He sat down at the kitchen table and wiped his eyes with a paper napkin. "Arrangements. I'm supposed to discuss the arrangements with some undertaker guy and Aunt Ethel. Flowers, music, photographs. What do I know about that stuff?"

"Have a beer," Frank offered but Mikey pushed the can aside and crossing his arms on the table buried his face.

When Gina entered the bedroom Rita was seated at a small dressing table putting the finishing touches on her make-up. She was wearing a denim dress, stockings and high heeled shoes and seemed in a hurry to leave the apartment.

"We're going to have our pictures taken in half an hour so fix your hair and do your face," she told Gina and moved from the dressing table to sit on the edge of the bed.

Gina did as she was told while Rita talked on about how Aunt Ethel and Mr. Henderson were going to put together photos in a heart shaped frame, the baby in the center surrounded by her grandparents, Gina and her mother. And then there were other things to be done: a check mailed to the cemetery and a baby dress bought and delivered to Mr. Henderson.

As Rita's voice grew increasingly shrill, Gina spun round on the stool to face her.

"Take it easy. Mikey ought to have a say."

Rita shivered and wrapped her arms tightly around her upper body. "Mikey says the arrangements are a lot of crap. At first, he was all excited by the idea that she had his blue eyes. Now that she's dead he doesn't want to see her. He's afraid she'll look gross, full of holes and bruises." Rita crumpled and fell sideways face down on the bed. "She'll look beautiful, just perfect. Aunt Ethel promised."

Gina let her cry.

Aunt Ethel kept her promise. Baby Gina in her white coffin was unblemished. "A little flower among flowers," one of the regulars whispered to her friend as they admired the floral arrangements in Mr. Henderson's chapel. Mikey and Frank had left Albany before the funeral but the ceremony had been well attended by ladies of a certain age whose comments told Gina that they went to such functions frequently and were qualified to judge the quality of the arrangements. After the burial Aunt Ethel invited special friends back to her apartment for sandwiches and coffee. Rita had helped in the beauty salon at the beginning of her stay in Albany and knew many of these silver haired ladies who gathered around her. They moved slowly and filled the room with an easy murmur of consoling phrases that required no response. Rita, caught in the ebb and flow of their voices, looked calm. She stood with her back to the mantelpiece, nodded and wiped her eyes occasionally as a special friend took her hand or kissed her cheek.

"Rita dear, you must stay. Ethel is getting on. She needs you in the salon," Gina heard a bent-over ash blonde say.

"I'll think about it," Rita replied.

Once Gina returned home Frank came over most evenings. Mikey usually followed with more than a couple of drinks under his belt. The summer was suddenly over. The evenings were too cool to sit in the Pontiac. Frank hadn't had time to repair the heater which in any case required running the motor and consuming gas for the sake of sitting uncomfortably three abreast in the front seat. So Gina's parents stayed out of the way and left them the living room.

"When's Rita coming back?" Mikey would ask Gina as he settled with a beer on the sofa opposite the TV. "How come you don't know? You're her best friend."

"I don't think she has made up her mind," Gina would reply and then ask Frank what he and Mikey had planned for the evening. These days they never had any definite plans and left it to her to decide whether to go out or stay in. As a rule they ended up in front of the TV where Mikey dozed and she and Frank argued about what program to watch.

Three weeks after her return Gina received a note and colored photos in a heart shaped gilt frame. Rita wrote that she liked working with hair and was attracting some younger women to the salon who were becoming her friends as well as her regulars. Gina stood the frame upright on the coffee table in front of the sofa where Frank and Mikey always sat facing the TV.

Frank arrived early to watch interviews and reruns of historic plays before the live football game began.

"Got any Fritos?" he asked pushing the picture frame to one side.

Gina placed a bowl of peanuts on the coffee table. "This came today from Rita." She pointed to the picture frame.

Frank pondered the photos in the shifting light of the TV. "She's put everybody in but Mikey," he said sourly.

"Mikey blew it in Albany. You both blew it."

"Before Albany the only dead person we had ever seen was Mikey's grandfather and he was eighty-six years old."

"That baby wasn't dead the first time you saw her," Gina said raising her voice over the chatter of the sports commentators.

"No, she was a bunch of tubes. Now for Christ's sake hide that thing away before Mikey sees it."

Gina picked up the picture frame.

"Hi, guys," Mikey, a six pack under his arm, came in and stood in front of the set. A football soared end over end above a field. "That was one hell of a play," he shouted along with the screaming fans.

The ball dropped between the goal posts and disappeared, crowded off the screen by two babies seated in a slowly rotating tire. Gina loved the Michelin commercial. Frank and Mikey despised it. They claimed the tires were fake. They worked with cars and could tell. Maybe the babies were fakes, too. Made out of rubber and plastic.

"Zap 'em," Mikey said and went into the kitchen.

Gina followed him and held the refrigerator door open while he pulled the beer cans out of the plastic strapping and tried to line them up on the top shelf. He had been drinking and two of the cans slipped out of his hand onto the floor.

When he had finished she closed the door and said, "Rita sent me this."

He took the picture frame from her, held it up to the light and examined the photos one by one, focusing finally on that of the baby in the center. Then he ran his right index finger slowly around the edge of the baby picture touching the rim of the white coffin here and a bit of white satin there and when his hand began to shake he laid the frame down flat on the table and bent over it. "You and Rita look terrific in those summer dresses. When she comes back the four of us will celebrate. We'll rent skates and go ice skating at Rockefeller Center."

"Mikey, Rita isn't coming back."

He stood rigidly upright and steadied himself against the table. "You're a couple of bullshit artists, you and Rita. That kid, even if she did have blue eyes, she wasn't mine."

"Hey, Mikey. The game is about to start." Frank came into the kitchen.

"I'll watch it with the guys at Louie's. See you around." He walked passed Frank into the living room.

"You showed it to him," Frank said.

"Yes, and I told him Rita isn't coming back." Gina grabbed the picture frame off the table.

As he came toward her and raised his hand she closed her eyes and screamed.

"What's going on, Frankie boy? Come on to Louie's. Bring money. The guys will be betting big bucks."

Mikey swayed boozily in the kitchen doorway.

Frank turned and looked at him. "Nothing's going on but I'm taking a bet right here, one hundred to one, Gina's going to move in with Rita and they'll both do hair and marry rich guys in black suits and gloves."

Mikey braced himself sideways in the door frame and slid to the floor. "And have babies in tires." He laughed helplessly.

Gina stepped over him, and went to her bedroom. A moment later after the front door slammed she returned to the living room and stood for a moment in front of the TV. A pile of brightly uniformed bodies glistened on green turf. She and Rita never watched football. Mikey and Frank had made it clear they preferred to watch without them. Now she was charmed by the grace and order with which the layers of bodies peeled off the pile down to the last man who lay curled up, hugging the ball. It was a fairy tale. A flower opened petal by petal and there at the heart of the rose the hero held the treasure. She switched the set off. During the commercial, Mikey and Frank would be telling the guys about a couple of girls married to undertakers and giving birth to plastic babies. A pathetic joke but Frank had given her a good idea.

"I'm on my way," she wrote Rita. "I might never have thought of it without him."

The River's Story

AT SUMMER'S END fields thirst. The river bed is dry, the river silent, dead. Flowers die, birds depart and trees, touched by frost turn gaudy as tarts but without birds they are mute until rain arrives and the river's rise is heard in the leaves.

Clean Up

THE SUN was a yellow patch on a sky as gray as an unwashed sheet streaked with dirty clouds, all darkening, sinking from sight.

Suddenly stars every one believed burnt out appeared and winked and blinked and twinkled all night.

By morning the mess had been cleaned up.

The Listeners ℘

"THEY LIKE MOZART BEST," she said from her dark corner of the loft and immediately thereafter regretted having spoken. Given the state of his nerves, it was foolhardy to draw his attention to the secret listeners of his playing. Sometimes, the mere thought of a live audience paralyzed him. Fortunately at the moment he stood under a harsh fluorescent light and was too absorbed in studying the score of Beethoven's violin concerto on the stand in front of him to have caught her words about them, the Mozart lovers who shared the shadows with her and listened intently, their round eyes bright and unblinking, their heads slightly cocked as Mozart's Concerto in A Major filled the dusty air of the loft. Not that they appeared unmoved by the Beethoven which he played with equal brilliance. Perhaps it was Mozart's tenderness, a delicacy rising from such deep strength in the Adagio that captivated them as it did her.

She had seen something of that sensitivity in his pale features and tall narrow frame the first time she heard him play. They had met seated side by side in the cheapest seats at a concert in Carnegie Hall. She was new to the city and lonely so when he invited her to his place to hear him play she accepted. His place was in an old warehouse, one bleak room furnished with three chairs and a table from the Salvation Army. There he had played the Mozart A major and Beethoven D minor for her, the violin concerti he was to perform in public in six weeks.

"It will be a second debut for me. I was a prodigy, a *wunderkind.* I relished performing on stage but at my New York debut at the age of eight I froze, just stood and stared at rows upon rows of faces. Finally Menuhin stepped down from the podium and guided me off stage. Even now after fifteen years there are moments when I panic at the thought of being listened to by a live audience."

As the date for his "second debut" drew nearer, he recounted the haunting memory over and over in a voice tinged with hysteria. She tried to ease his anxiety and relieve his isolation. She was not gifted musically. No perfect pitch, no ear-hand coordination. Her talent, her only talent, she believed, was to be quiet, part of the silence, a listening presence. He practiced to the point of exhaustion. On her return from her book-keeper's job, she would find him collapsed in a chair staring at the yellow-gray ceiling. He saw no one. The silence in the loft was absolute. Not a sound from within the old warehouse or from the streets penetrated the thick walls. He needed the emptiness, the noiseless vacuum. At times, the loneliness seemed more than she could bear and then she found consolation in the music and the company of the secret listeners who shared her unlit corner. They didn't always appear; there was no telling why, and she worried. They were timid music lovers. At a jarring sound, they would scurry away.

On Saturdays, the only time he left the loft, he went to his teacher, Emilio Baroni. She could tell if the session had gone well by his mood on his return. This Saturday, it had gone very well. He was happily excited.

"After the concert, we'll escape to the country for awhile. Now I will play for you," he said taking his place in the icily lit patch in the dark loft.

She sat with her eyes half-closed and let the music refresh her spirit. Along the nearby wall, her fellow listeners gathered, one by one, in a silvery line.

"I love you," she said softly when he had finished.

"You will always be my only audience. In the concert hall I will see only your face," he promised.

On the elevator door, a piece of cardboard scrawled in pencil said "Out Of Order" as it had three days before when she had rushed to Long Island to look after her ailing mother. She wished he had warned her that she would have to climb the fire stairs. She would have asked him to come down and help carry her suitcase but when she had phoned him from the bus station to say she had arrived back in the city, his voice had been edgy, his words unfocused.

She picked up her suitcase and started up the steep

fire stairs. A naked red bulb at each landing was the only light. When she reached the fourth floor she stopped. From the half open door of the loft came the strains of Mozart's Adagio. A streak of bluish fluorescent light marked the floor. For a moment she hesitated on the landing, afraid to interrupt him.

The playing suddenly stopped. "*Da capo* dammit," he shouted and began at the beginning only to stop again.

She slipped into the moment of silence and entered the room.

Pale and unshaven, he peered out beneath the shaft of overhead light. She attempted to tip toe silently to her chair but crumbs crunched on the bare floor like gravel under foot.

"Please go on playing," she said and sat down in her usual corner.

Never had his playing held her so completely. In his hands the violin became a soaring voice that filled the loft with a grave sweetness.

She longed to applaud, to express her elation. She searched the shadows for those who had listened with her in the past. They were not in their usual place. She leaned forward toward the wall. An irregular silver-gray line ran along the baseboard.

"What have you done?" she cried as she made out a series of tiny corpses in traps.

He lifted the bow from the strings and called over to her, "Rats. They came out whenever I played. I couldn't stand it."

"Mice, not rats. Harmless little mice. They listened with me."

"*Da capo*," he muttered and resumed playing, starting with the opening bars of the Adagio.

"Brilliant, Outstanding" she read in the papers and was glad for him. She had not used the ticket he had sent her and she did not save the clippings of the reviews.

Wide Awake ✍

THE DOCTOR in the white coat said, "It will be some time before I can get to your Dinah. There are so many in need. They come from the world over."

He pointed to the waiting Oriental ladies with elaborate ornaments in their black hair, Navajo women in red velvet blouses, black African babies, a few dimpled Kewpies as well as prettily dressed girls with dainty porcelain hands and faces. The layers of dust that dulled their faces and finery proved that all had been at the clinic a very long time, crowded together, some seated, some toppled, arms and legs askew. However, in spite of the long uncomfortable wait, each one was wide awake. Rows upon rows of wide open eyes stared fixedly, locked in the moment of loss: the fall, break crack cut.

"I'll do my best," the doctor promised as he placed Dinah on a shelf next to an Eskimo boy.

She sat primly upright, her severed leg cradled in her lap, her eyes no longer meeting mine but joining the common gaze.

Outside the Good as New Clinic I saw a small bare-foot girl coming in my direction. She clutched a little doll, a bunch of rags tied with string. The brown wood head was crudely carved, the features incised in black. At first I thought she might be bringing it to the clinic. But no, she passed me by and was gripping the doll so tightly by its neck that I cried out, "Be careful, you'll choke her."

She looked at me with tar black eyes too big for her emaciated face and then hurried after a man on a foot-path that meandered away from the road into the brush. The path died in a field barren except for clumps of spiky weeds that put forth tiny crimson blossoms fine as needles.

The man appeared familiar with the place for he walked directly to a shallow depression where the raw earth had settled above some sort of pit. After a few steps he stopped and pointed to a place at his feet. The girl squatted beside the spot and with her free hand attempted to dig in the hard baked soil. The man, seeing that she could only scratch the surface, bent over and drew a bone about the length of his forearm from under his ragged cloak. He handed it to the girl.

She dug into the ground with such a fury that for a moment she disappeared in swirls of dust. Once the dust settled she held the doll above the hole and with a single blow severed it at the neck. She tossed the head in after the body and covered them with dirt. Then she and the man walked into the bush.

The doctor was still working on the Balinese dancer's bejewelled broken ankle.

When he noticed me standing in the doorway, he said gruffly, "I told you this morning I'm very busy. People like you want miracles."

"I'll bring her back another time," I lied and lifted Dinah and her leg down off the shelf. The Eskimo boy fell forward on his face.

Here at home Dinah and I rest on a pile of pillows. The severed leg is under the bed. Since she is wearing a long satin nightdress its absence is not noticeable. As I brush the dust from her hair she fixes me with a gaze dark, deep as a hole a child could fall into.

Calcutta Connections 🙊

> "Imparadised in one another's arms"
> Milton, *Paradise Lost*

> "We are the world."
> Theme song of famine relief drive

"THERE'S AN ARROW sticking out of your ribs," he says fondling her naked breasts. "I never noticed it before."

"It was in too deep. Now it's working its way out like a big sliver and I barely feel it." She kisses him and moves his hands elsewhere.

"Who shot you?" he asks after they have made love.

"Mother Teresa."

"Mother Teresa of Calcutta, the nun who collects dying children off the streets?"

"That's the one."

"But you've never been to Calcutta."

"I was an innocent by-stander right here on Main Street, U.S.A. The arrow had ricocheted off Mount Everest and it hit me as I came out of the supermarket. I wrote Mother Teresa and complained. She replied that there is no such creature as an innocent by-stander. For every dying child she sends a prayer to heaven and shoots an arrow into the sky."

"She's a regular Rambo," he says acidly.

Making love while that arrow protrudes is awkward. He fears accidentally driving the metal tip back in. She is distracted by the cries of babies dying in Calcutta. Sometimes he and she part frustrated and angry.

One afternoon he offers to help her remove the hindrance. She closes her eyes and together they give a little tug. The arrow pops out as easily as a loose baby tooth and takes with it echoes of baby cries.

"At last you and I can get back in sync," he cheers and kisses away the scar above her heart.

"Good-bye Calcutta," she cheers.

Imparadised in one another's arms they sink onto the bed, its flowered spread and spacious king size their Eden. They are in sync. No one else exists.

"We are the world," they whisper.

When they come to rest and lie side by side she says, "Bob suspects us."

"Marsha too," he sighs.

They are saddened. They have taken every precaution, timed their phone calls carefully to arrange meetings in remote motels. She always wears dark glasses and a scarf on her head.

"We don't want to hurt Bob and Marsha and there are the children to consider. We mustn't hurt any of them," he broods.

When she agrees saying, "There's already too much

pain in the world," he counters, "Don't start that Mother Teresa of Calcutta crap again."

"What *are* you talking about? I've never been to Calcutta."

To allay the suspicions of their spouses they agree to postpone seeing each other for two weeks.

She arrives promptly. The place calls itself an inn but the room is identical to all other motel rooms they have stayed in except that he isn't in it. She leaves the door open a crack and takes off her dark glasses and scarf. He is late. Cars pull in and out of the parking lot. There is no sign of his Chrysler. She turns on the TV. A child, all eyes and belly, fills the screen. She paces around the room.

"How can he be late? He's never late."

The child is silent. Its eyes track her.

"Sorry, kid. I've never been to the Sahara or Somalia. The only place I go is to the supermarket where I shop for Bob and the twins."

Outside in the parking lot a car door slams. She rushes to the door. He is pale and walks stiffly. The instant he crosses the threshold she takes his face in both hands and kisses him. His mouth has a bitter taste.

"You're late. I worried."

She wraps her arms around him. He winces.

They are not in sync.

"I've been hit," he gasps.

Her hand meets the shaft freshly embedded between his shoulder blades.

"Leave me be," he says and collapses face down on the king-sized bed.

She dashes from the room.

Above the parking lot the evening sky is studded with starbright arrowheads. She looks back into the room. It is empty except for a throng of naked children who squat on the bed. Behind them his pale face bobs up and down as he picks spent arrows off the ground and puts them in a brown paper shopping bag.

Stay Tuned ✍

TOM WAITED on the steps of the cabin, the Chevy keys clenched in his sweaty hand, his eyes fixed on his mother and father who stood at the edge of the lake. They did that every evening, walked the hundred yards through the weeds to the shore and watched the sunset. What they did the rest of the time he had no idea. Since arriving at the lake three weeks ago he had steered clear of them, slept late, grabbed something from the refrigerator and then asked his father if he could take the Chevy with the excuse that he wanted to explore the area and familiarize himself with the Grenville campus where he was to be a freshman in September. The college was twenty miles to the north but he never drove further than the nearby town of Lakeside where he hung around the bowling alley or, if the weather wasn't stinking hot, he joined some of the local high school kids to shoot baskets in the park. Even in the lousy hick town of Lakeside in the middle of Rhode Island they had heard of the Sabers, the Capitol high school champs from Washington, D.C. A couple of the guys, sports fanatics, recognized him as having been a member of the team. Sometimes his parents needed the car to go to the supermarket, the *only* place they ever went, and then he walked the four miles through the woods to the highway and hitched a ride. However, most days, his father simply nodded at the car keys that hung on the nail inside the screen door and then immersed himself in his book. Every summer at the start of his vacation his father made a list of books in the field of American history and read through it until the next August when he compiled a new list. This summer the topic was Jefferson.

His parents referred to these weeks at the lake as a great vacation away from the August heat of Washington.

The cabin belonged to Uncle Fred, his father's younger brother, the star of the family, a meteorologist with the E.P.A. and a frequent guest on TV talk shows to explain the greenhouse effect, acid rain and other man-made catastrophes. The TV camera loved him and as one TV host noted, his affable manner took the hysteria out of environmental doomsday.

In addition to being talkative Uncle Fred was very tall and friends of the family would remark, "Tom, you sure take after your Uncle Fred." When he had objected angrily to his mother that they had nothing in common she had replied, "Don't take on. You're the son he would have liked."

Uncle Fred had two daughters and at the end of July had said, "I don't have much use for the cottage now that my girls are on their own, Deb in law school and Diane in a training program at a large New York bank."

He hated Uncle Fred and his white Honda Accord and his superachieving daughters, especially Deb who patronized him for his high school athletic record with, "So, another big black boy slam dunks a basketball."

"Go study your torts and get off my back," he told her.

He loved the game, loved being good, very good at it but he always knew it was a game and he would make his life off the basketball court, exactly how or where he wished he knew. He hadn't yet figured it out and resented being pressured.

One day when Deb continued to nag him with "Where's the big boy headed these days?" he had turned on her.

"Okay, Miss Minority Affirmative Action law school student."

He knew Deb was extremely sensitive about not being identified as someone who had been accepted at Yale for reasons other than her academic record. She not only did not need help because she was female and African American, she did not need financial aid of any kind. Her parents were paying the full tuition.

After a harsh exchange they had made up but he had remained unreconciled to Uncle Fred. Most of all he resented his father's accepting "the cottage" – Uncle Fred's word for the crummy cabin – rent free.

"You don't owe me a cent. Enjoy."

"Oh, I'm sure we will," his mother had said with her

fourth grade teacher optimism. "And Grenville, Tom's college is in the area which means we can help him move his hi-fi and his bike from there instead of having to drive up from Washington."

His mother had placed the emphasis on him and avoided any mention of the fact that with his father just laid off his job as assistant manager of a printing company, the cabin rent free came as a blessing.

This evening they lingered longer than usual by the water, this evening just when he needed to tell his father about the accident – nobody hurt but the Chevy's front fender bashed in when two Chicanos in a pick-up with Texas plates side-swiped him, yelled something, first in Spanish, then "Off the road, black boy," and drove on. He had had a few beers and since he was six months short of eighteen had chucked the cans out in case some trooper drove up and noticed him puking in the ditch along side the battered Chevy. Nobody had come, the car ran okay, and he had parked it in the woods near the cabin but out of sight until he could talk to his father. He knew his father would insist on the car going to the body shop for repairs immediately even though that left them all without wheels. The car was old but well-maintained. His parents wouldn't be seen driving a beat-up Chevy like a couple of blue collar migrants come north looking for work.

Now they turned from the shore and walked slightly bent into their shadows, stepping cautiously to avoid thistles. With the last flare of sunlight at their backs, they looked as if they had emerged from the lake, two ebony figures touched with gold, two ancient masks, eyes half-closed.

Suddenly, unable to face them, he took two hundred and fifty dollars from his wallet, savings from his Christmas and graduation money, and leaving it and the car keys on the porch steps, he dashed through the woods to the interstate.

Several cars passed him. Finally a van stopped. The driver was a deaf, garrulous black man, a chicken farmer from up-state.

"I go past Grenville College, glad to drop you off," he shouted. "Hitching is dangerous, especially at night, even for a big fellow like you. I always carry a shotgun" – he pointed to the gun rack behind the seat – "Drive with the doors locked. From what I hear there's some pretty weird things happening on college campuses these days. Grenville's mostly white, some black kids. You a student there?"

"I ain't no janitor," he drawled and then yelled, "Yeah, freshman. There's the gate. I'll walk in."

"You take care," the old man said and let him off on the side of the road.

He had visited the college once with his father when he had come for an interview but now in the darkness the campus grounds were unfamiliar. Clusters of white globes mounted on black cast iron lampposts shed dim light on winding footpaths. The buildings screened by the dark foliage of trees and shrubs were silent. He kept to the main driveway that led from the gate at the campus entrance to a flood-lit brick building with a white cupola, the library. When his father had admired the architecture noting the influence of Monticello, he had reacted in a mean-spirited manner calling Jefferson a slave owner, the father of two illegitimate children by Sally Henning.

"That has no bearing on the architecture," his father had replied evenly.

Now for want of any other landmark he walked slowly toward the domed building staying in the shadows fearful of being spotted by a security guard. He passed several cars parked on the side of the road. A cream-colored Subaru wagon caught his eye. The back seat was down, the trunk unlocked. He climbed in. A tight fit for his six foot seven. He drew his knees to his chest and fell asleep.

"You homeless?"

The girl was peering at him through the open door by the driver's seat. A beautiful black face, topaz eyes, the girl drew the morning light to her and warmed it.

"You a homeless person or sleeping something off?" she asked more sharply.

"Not exactly." He struggled feet first out of the trunk door and hurriedly stuffed his T shirt into his jeans. "I'm a freshman. Since this place was closed down tight last night I thought you wouldn't mind." He came and stood opposite her.

She was a small girl. He slouched down to disguise his height. She shut the car door.

"Neat wagon," he said and patted the roof slippery with morning dew.

"You travel light." She looked him up and down.

He read his messy scared image in her eyes: a runaway, drugs, wanted by the cops.

"My folks are bringing my things by car."

"Seems you don't read your mail. Seniors move in today. Freshmen aren't due until next week."

She turned and walked across the street to a red brick building with a white portico. A sign on one of the columns read "Administration."

"Wait," he called and followed her to the steps.

From the top step she confronted him at eye level and waited.

"My name is Thomas Jackson. I graduated from Columbia High, Washington, D.C. It's a terrific school. Maybe you've heard of it."

She shook her head. Her glossy black hair floated away from her face.

"Our basketball team won the championship. I've got a scholarship here."

The rush of words echoed loudly in his ears but her expression was so blank he wondered if she could hear him.

Finally she said, "Grenville doesn't give athletic scholarships. No black athlete would consider us. Don't get me wrong. We're committed to our minority students but as a small college we have a limited budget for sports. Our guys play soccer, tennis."

"You got me wrong," he mimicked her angrily. "I'm not coming to play white boy's tennis or black man's basketball. I have the Hamilton scholarship for academic excellence."

She was silent for a moment, her features immobile. Then her face came alive as she laughed and clasped her hands together.

"I didn't mean to hassle you but I have no way of knowing that some tall guy who arrives days ahead of schedule without even a change of socks is one of our scholars. Glad to meet you. I'm Beverly Parsons, one of the assistant deans."

She smiled. The most beautiful girl he had ever seen was smiling at him. To be nearer he took the three steps in one stride. When she drew away from his towering over her, he stopped short and slumped against a column.

"I came early because the scholarship covers only tuition. Seeing as how you're an assistant dean maybe you ought to help me find a place to live and a job so I won't be a homeless black bum on campus while your guys are playing soccer."

She came over to him.

"Knock that chip off your shoulder, Thomas Jackson. You're part of Grenville now so get your head together. Like it or not you're New South moved North, middle class. Understand what I'm telling you? We're high profile, a minority within a minority."

He thought of Uncle Fred and glared at her.

She glared back. "Don't you go messing us up behaving like some ghetto kid who never had a chance."

He thought of the Chevy in the shop, his parents alone by the lake.

A couple of workmen moving file cabinets on a dolly

clattered out of the front door of the building. When they had passed she motioned him to follow her inside.

"See Mrs. Shaun, room 110." She looked at her watch and laughed softly. "You're always ahead of schedule. The offices don't open till nine but Mrs. Shaun is usually at her desk early. Say I sent you."

Room 110 was at the end of a long vaulted corridor. A glazed glass door opened into a square room lined with file cabinets on one side. Opposite, tall windows looked out on four empty tennis courts. The room was very quiet and empty except for two women who sat at facing grey steel desks behind a panelled counter. One woman was black, the other Oriental. Where the hell were all the whites? he wondered. Both looked up at the squeak of his hi-top Reeboks on the rubber tile floor.

"Beverly Parsons sent me to see Mrs. Shaun," he said and was relieved when it was the black woman who got up from her desk and came over to the counter.

"How may I help you?" she asked.

The courtesy and Southern softness in her voice made him so suddenly homesick he could barely state his name. She motioned him around the counter to a chair beside her desk and when she repeated her offer of help he blurted that he needed a place to live. His tuition was paid for. Yes, he had a scholarship but no money for room and board.

"I can't ask my folks," he lied but he would have felt like a traitor telling a stranger, even a sympathetic lady like Mrs. Shaun, that his father was unemployed. "My folks are very old. They would like to help but they're really old."

"I understand," Mrs. Shaun murmured and getting up from her desk went across the room to a file cabinet.

The Oriental lady – was she Korean or Indonesian or maybe Vietnamese? – sat motionless in front of a bar graph on the screen of her computer.

He stared out the window at the tennis courts. Uncle Fred played tennis at a Washington country club and had tried to teach him the fine points of the game.

"This is not a slugger's sport, Tommy. Finesse, style, control count."

After listening to his uncle's lectures on Arthur Ashe's intelligent strategy and Billie Jean King's elegant drop shot he erupted on the court, pounded the ball, grunted at every stroke.

He won the game; his uncle took the match saying, "You're out of control, boy."

Tennis wasn't his game. He missed the team work, the total involvement and physical release of basketball.

The tennis racquet might as well have been an axe, the ball with its white fuzzy skin a badly peeled orange at which he slashed, chopped and over hit, unable to focus his energy. Now at the sight of the courts and the soccer field beyond he felt himself losing control. In a panic he was ready to bolt but Mrs. Shaun, returning to her desk, was between him and the door.

"The Hamilton scholarship is very distinguished."

She leafed through papers in a manila folder. "Your parents must be very proud of you."

"Yes, they are. My dad liked the campus, especially the library. He reads a lot."

"According to this," Mrs. Shaun pulled a blue sheet out of the folder, "Your father has paid your room and board for the first semester. He sent us a check a few weeks ago."

His father's severance pay, savings, a loan from Uncle Fred? He stared into the waste basket. In his head Beverly Parsons was saying, "You're messing up, Jackson. How come you don't communicate with your folks?"

"The room assignments for freshmen will be ready next week," Mrs. Shaun smiled.

"I'll come back. Thanks." He edged away from the desk.

"We'll see you then. By the way, your folks aren't so old. Our records show your father is only forty-three. Maybe that seems ancient to someone seventeen."

Her gentle laughter followed him out of the room and was lost in the ringing of the telephones and buzz of voices that issued from the offices that lined the corridor. He dashed out the main door, dodging incoming bodies with briefcases.

"Hi, Tommy," a voice called from somewhere beyond the portico. "He's my nephew, a great kid, fine athlete, terrific student."

"We have met," Beverly Parsons replied. She was standing beside Uncle Fred who was half-seated on the gleaming front fender of the Honda. "We met earlier this morning. You're a talented family."

"The real brains are over there in front of the library. Tommy gets his from his father. Now about that seminar on acid rain."

He hurried past them and joined his father.

"'I have sworn,'" his father read softly to himself the gold incised words that girdled the base of the cupola.

"I'm sorry about the Chevy, Dad."

"It will be okay. I worried about you."

"I'm okay."

His father continued to read while circling the building. "'I have sworn upon the altar of God eternal hostility to any form of tyranny over the mind of man.'"

"Do you know who said that?" his father asked.

"Sure. Judy Holiday in *Born Yesterday*. We watched it together on late TV."

"Yes, I remember. Thanks to her Thomas Jefferson has found a vast new audience," his father laughed softly.

They returned to the front of the building.

"How come you and Uncle Fred are here? What's going on?"

"I figured you had hitched a ride last night and then couldn't get home. Your uncle stopped by the cabin on his way from a lecture in Providence and offered to drive me here. That young woman he is talking to recognized him as soon as we got out of the car to look for you."

"Are they friends?" he asked.

Uncle Fred was smiling and gesticulating. Beverly Parsons was listening and nodding. The sun reflected off the Honda's white surface joined them in a glassy light.

"They met at some conference he chaired in Atlanta. She told us you were in the administration building."

"Did she tell you I slept in her car last night?"

His father gave him a pained look and then said quickly, "She did not."

"Bye," Beverly Parsons waved and disappeared down a treelined path.

"Let's go, guys," Uncle Fred called.

He sat in the center of the back seat so he could concentrate on the road and ignore the voices up front. As they pulled out of the campus gate, sound exploded from the Honda's four speakers. He recognized the tape.

"Let me know if it's too warm back there," Uncle Fred shouted.

Frigid air poured from the hidden vents.

"'I know that my redeemer liveth.' I know the ice age will get us all," he hummed with the tape and the air conditioning, then closed his eyes and slept.

He woke with a shiver. "Highlights of Handel" had run its course but a draft of chilling air was boring into his left shoulder. He slid over behind his father.

Uncle Fred was driving and speaking slowly.

"Sure the job market is tight but with your brains you've got nothing to worry about and Tommy will do fine which is more than I can say for my Deb."

"She's in law school."

"Was. All she's in now is trouble. The last time she and I communicated she accused me of being a coward.

It seems I avoid facing today's crises of race and sex discrimination by focusing on remote cosmic disaster. I'm out of touch with reality. I belong on the Cosby show."

Uncle Fred stepped on the accelerator and the Honda sped into the inside lane.

"I read somewhere that Bill Cosby and his wife donated a lot of money to education," his father said pleasantly.

"They did but according to Deb the TV show is a racist conspiracy to depict African Americans in terms of white bourgeois values. Hear that, Tommy? Do you ever watch the Cosby show?"

"Sure. It's harmless sitcom slush."

The chance to put down Deb was too good to miss but when the only reaction from the front seat was a shrug of his father's thin shoulders, he felt it had been a cheap shot against Cosby.

The road sign "Entering Lakeside Alt. 325" reminded his father that he needed to stop for groceries. "Just up ahead." He pointed to a small building with yellow plastic shingles. On the roof, a large red neon sign blinked "Lakeside Superette" at the sun. "You and Tom can wait in the diner next door. I won't be long."

The diner was empty. The teenager on a stool behind the counter was absorbed in the study of her fingernails.

"One coke with extra ice and a shake with three scoops of vanilla," Uncle Fred called from the booth.

"Okey dokey." The girl jumped off the stool. Long

rhinestone earrings glittered in and out of strands of blonde hair.

"How are things, Tommy?" Uncle Fred asked, scrutinizing him from across the table. "We're family and if you've got problems, I'm here to listen. Your dad, I really love that guy, has a lot on his mind right now."

"Thanks. I'm fine." He was thirsty, tired from sleeping in a car and now pressure was building. It was tennis all over again. Uncle Fred opposite him, filling the space.

To relieve the tension he said, "She's got probs. Probably never made a shake before." He nodded toward the counter where the girl was having trouble assembling the ingredients but Uncle Fred wanted to know what had happened with the Chevy.

He explained about the two guys in the pick-up. "I should have chased the bastards."

"Enjoy." The blonde smiled and gingerly placed the Coke and shake in the middle of the table.

"I should have beat the shit out of them."

"You should have told your dad," Uncle Fred said, chewing bits of ice from the Coke.

"But I didn't," he lashed out in exasperation. "No control, no guts. I can't handle your ozone and unlike Deb I don't hate Bill Cosby and his unreal TV world." He jabbed at the ice cream with a spoon sending it to the bottom of the tapered glass. White foam surged to the top and dribbled over the rim. "The glaciers are melting, oceans are overflowing and you and Deb and Beverly Parsons and all the other gutsy people will have to control the tides because I'm sure to screw up."

"Try cleaning up that mess for starters." Uncle Fred pushed a paper napkin across the table.

His father came in the diner, a bag of groceries in each arm. "I phoned your mother so she wouldn't worry," he said coming over to the booth. "And Fred, Deb has suddenly appeared at the cabin looking for you. I'll wait in the car. We ought to get going. They are preparing a picnic lunch."

"Terrific." Tom burst out and slapped the table. "Picnic by the lake. We're the super sitcom family."

"Right," Uncle Fred laughed, grabbed his hand and pulled him out of the booth. "And today maybe my daughter will give me a second chance at reality. Stay tuned, girl." He tossed the check with some money on the counter and did a sort of soft shoe out the door.

The girl giggled and hurried over to Tom. "I've seen your friend, the tall one, on TV. Right?"

"Right. My Uncle Fred. He's Bill Cosby's brother."

"Wow. Then you must be Bill Cosby's...."

He left her trying to puzzle it out while she sponged vanilla ice cream off the table top.

The Girl and Boy 🐾

SENTIMENTAL TOURISTS from up-state, we walk arm in arm through the New York Historical, the Metropolitan, the Guggenheim, MOMA, the Brooklyn plus Bridge, Asia Society, China Institute, Cooper-Hewitt, Morgan, Frick.

There is no museum, no art in our hometown. This trip, a second honeymoon, is intended to refresh our spirits, rekindle old fires after ten years of marriage.

Hand in hand we stand before Raphael's Madonna, her flesh aglow beneath veils. Goya's sublimely naked Maia—"on loan"—observes us from a bed. But Beauty has not ignited us. We feel inadequate, unable to rise to the occasion.

At each day's end we return exhausted to the hotel and write postcards home, full color reproductions of beautiful paintings.

This afternoon we "do" the last museum on our list, the Natural History, and as we head footsore for the exit the girl and boy catch our eye. They lie under glass exposed to public view and so interlaced it would be a futile game of Pick-up Sticks to separate the skeletons.

I stand transfixed by the impassioned embrace "pre-served in Himalayan ice for a millennium," the museum label states.

You circle the case, discover cracks, minute as flaws in porcelain, threading the two craniums: signs of ritual homicide, death without disfigurement.

We agree that these lovers were supposed to kneel side by side in chastity, a sacrifice to appease the lust of monumental gods now ranged—"new acquisitions"— against a mural of the glacial site. From raw peaks beneath a blanched sky they stare through us, their wide, stone eyes wedded to the play of incandescent limbs annealed in a translucent bed.

"Closing time," a guard calls.

Once outside we walk apart lest our joined hands ignite in a public place.

Minna's Woods 🌿

"Look out there at the woods," Minna said.

"Yes, dear," Linda replied but she was too busy preparing supper to give more than a quick glance out the kitchen window at her mother-in-law's insistence. "I see the boys have left their toys all over the yard again," she said and went back to washing a head of lettuce.

"Use the eyes God gave you and you'll see what I do," Minna ordered and left the kitchen for her room.

Linda went out on the back porch. As she peered beyond the toy cluttered yard to the edge of the woods the white against the gold caught her attention. A huge maple, its crest touched by the last rays of the sun, cast a shadow on the ground where the lamb lay nestled against the lion. In the fading light she could just make out the large amber eyes, the white muzzle sheltered in the golden ruff of the mane.

"You out there on the porch, hon?"

In an effort to hold the vision she closed her mind to his voice and the pop of a beer can.

"The boys and I could eat a horse."

At the touch of his cold wet fingers on the nape of her neck she shuddered.

"Supper's ready on the stove, Rob. Tell the children to get in their pajamas. I'll come in a minute."

The sudden hug of his arm around her shoulders almost lifted her off her feet and left her breathless. When she looked up again the maple stood in darkness above an even darker patch of empty ground.

The kitchen was stifling, the cool from the porch lost in the heat from the old cast iron stove.

"We could eat a horse couldn't we Dad?" Timmy, the younger of the two boys seated at the table, giggled.

"'Cept that it's tuna fish again," his brother John sighed over his plate.

"Okay, guys, no complaints about your mother's cooking. Clean your plates or you'll be weak as chicks when we wrestle."

"Try not to make too much noise, Rob. Your mother's asleep," Linda warned when he pushed away from the table and grabbed a squealing child under each arm. "And remember, once I've done the dishes it's bed time."

The kitchen floor boards vibrated with the thumps of bodies rough-housing in the parlor. The old farm house, once a single room cabin built by Minna's grandfather and added to by succeeding generations, was a jumble of small rooms, dark hallways, closets all patched together.

The voices grew louder, the laughter on the edge of tears. She pulled the plug in the sink and hurried to the parlor door. Rob lay on the floor and gripped Timmy between his thighs while his right arm pinned John face down across his chest. Flushed and breathless the boys pounded their small fists on his torso.

"Ow, owee," he groaned at each blow and slapped the floor with his free hand. "Ow, owee," the boys screamed.

At her "That's enough. It's bed time," all three bodies deflated in a tangle of limbs. John scrambled to his feet.

"Nite, Dad," he gasped between hiccups.

"Carry me, Mom," Timmy whined and remained squatting.

"Baby, baby," John teased and padded down the hall to the bedroom.

Timmy was heavy, all chest and arms like his father. When she leaned over to put him on the bed she felt a painful pull in her gut where the infant girl had died. She knelt down and eased him under the covers. He sighed drowsily at her kiss. From the next bed John tugged at her skirt. She sat down on the edge of the bed and held him in her arms.

"Hiccups gone?"

"Nope."

"I'll get you a glass of water."

Returning from the bathroom she stopped to look in on Minna. The old woman lay curled on her side, the bedding drawn tight around her small frame, her lined face against the pillow soft as if powdered white. The supper tray on the bedside table was untouched.

"She's dead, isn't she?" John whispered, squeezing against her in the doorway.

"She's asleep and you should be too. Come to bed. Your father is waiting for me."

"No, he isn't. He's watching T V. I can hear it."

"Drink your water and go to sleep."

Rob lay stretched out on the sofa, his feet hanging awkwardly over the end, his face sheltered against the garish TV light in the crook of one arm. She made her way quietly into the kitchen, turned off the light and then stood in the doorway to the porch. At night the woods seemed nearer, a dense fabric of black upon black. Tonight patches of white wove through the layers of darkness. Minna said that in the late summer the white tail deer came down from the hills, that she knew the path they followed and then she added in a dry voice, "We mustn't tell him. He has a gun."

"That you, Linda?" Rob mumbled and shifted his position exposing his face to the orange glare. The closed eyelids tightened, the chin with its shadow of a beard lowered against a collar bone. She turned off the set and then waited in the darkness to make sure he was still sleeping. He often fell asleep this way, flopped down exhausted from his long day at the Acme Feed and Equipment Co. in Clinton, but then he would wake with a start on the sofa and reach for her. At one time she had found pleasure and comfort in the strength of his body but since the stillbirth his lovemaking intensified the emptiness. At the rub of his face, rough against her cheek and breast, she longed for a tenderness lost when the dead body was taken from her, a girl baby, child of her heart, the one she dreamed to be forever gentle and quiet at her side. On the nights when she didn't respond to him he stomped out of the house, sat in the pick-up and drank beer with the headlights on and the radio blaring. It was only after he finally came to bed and fell asleep that she would inch close and take hold of one of his large hands.

Now as she took a coat from the back of the kitchen door and tip-toed over to cover him she froze. On the floor beside the sofa lay two guns and an open gun kit. He had promised never to bring guns into the house. She knew nothing about firearms, didn't dare touch them. Angry and frightened she gingerly placed the coat over them so that if one of the children did wake up – John had a habit of sneaking into the kitchen in the middle of the night – he wouldn't see them.

He rolled on his side and groped for Linda. Nothing. His hand dropped to the floor and he slipped back to sleep.

"Where am I? Where's Linda?"

The shrieks jolted him to open his eyes. In the gray morning light a figure wrapped in a bed sheet stood in the parlor doorway.

"For God's sake, Mother, go back to bed or you'll wake everyone." He swung his feet slowly to the floor so as not to frighten her.

She moved away one step at a time. "I don't know you. Why are you in my house?" she screamed and trailing the bedsheet disappeared down the dark hall.

He slumped back and closed his eyes. His mother hadn't recognized him for weeks. Some evenings when he arrived home dead tired she would see him in multiple images and cry out, "Why is my house full of strangers?" Only Linda could calm her. A word from Linda and she became docile. Linda treated her as if she were a small child and became a child herself. Together they sat on the porch like two little girls whispering secrets. Whenever his mother wandered into the woods in spite of his warnings, Linda frantic with worry stood with Timmy and John at the bottom of the yard yelling until she came out babbling nonsense about the old swing in the orchard.

"What's the matter with Gran?" the boys asked him.

"She's very old and gets confused."

"Why's she here with us?"

"We live here with her. The farm and this house belong to her."

"If she's so old maybe she'll die soon."

"I'm afraid she woke you," Linda's cool hand brushed his forehead. "She could harm herself in the dark. We'll have to get rails for the bed."

"Get anything you want, just so she leaves me alone. What time is it?" He rubbed his face with both hands and yawned.

"Almost five. I'll get your breakfast right away."

He reached up and took her hand. "Don't worry. I'm taking time off this week. It's deer season."

At the mention of deer hunting season, she saw again

a carcass hanging from the limb of the locust that grew off the back porch. The animal hung head down, its hind feet tied together. A trickle of blood dripped from the nose and as the carcass swung slowly around revealing the long gash in the white belly she had screamed, "Take that poor thing down, take it away and never bring your killings home again." Now a year later she had trouble keeping her voice under control as she said, "Those guns in there by the sofa, I was afraid they might be loaded." She placed a mug of coffee in front of him on the kitchen table.

"Of course they're not loaded. I was cleaning them. If you'd let me teach you to shoot you wouldn't be so scared."

"We've been over that before." She shrugged and returned to the stove. "Scrambled or fried?"

"Scrambled." He got up from his chair and stood next to her. "Maybe one of these mornings I'll take John with me, just to watch. At his age I learned a lot from my Dad."

Her body stiffened beside him. In the skillet the egg whites and yolks began to separate and harden but she made no move to stir them. He watched the edges of the mixture shrivel and then went on determined to make her understand.

"Hunting is part of growing up in the country. It takes skill, self-discipline."

"John can learn those things without killing," she said and left the kitchen.

He took the smoking skillet from the stove and placed it under running water in the sink.

Minna woke up feeling well and no longer afraid of the stranger with his guns she had seen in the dark parlor. She followed Linda about the house all morning telling her about the swing her father was building for her in the apple orchard.

"It's a birthday present, a swing with slatted benches facing each other."

"Yes I know, dear," Linda said as she wiped the kitchen counters. She had actually seen the swing one day when Rob had taken her and the boys into the woods. It had been neglected for years and was in such a decrepit condition that she had refused to let the boys ride in it until their father found time to rebuild it.

"And the deer came there at this time of year. They love the windfall apples," Minna continued although she saw that Linda's mind was elsewhere. Poor Linda, so bereaved, so busy, too busy with those boys, nice boys but rowdy, not quiet like the child, a delicate little thing who followed her through the woods, measuring its pace to her slow uncertain steps. She was always glad of the company, especially in the afternoons when the wind died down and she could wander along the deer paths or sit in the swing under the apple trees. They produced little fruit now and several, barren and skeletal, listed, exposing clotted roots, but those around the swing, although old and neglected, provided deep shade. The child, small and half hidden in the shadows that shifted with the cradling motion of the swing, would sit and listen while she closed her eyes and hummed nursery rhymes, hymns, whatever came into her head. Often she dozed off.

This afternoon she let the child lead the way deep into the woods. The sky, what little of it was visible through the trees, was darkened and the air had a bite. She reached down and took the child's hand. The tiny fingers felt thin and cold as if the bones were made of glass.

"Time to go home. Mustn't be late, Mamma worries," she said turning back.

The child resisted her.

"All right. Just a short while more."

The path under the trees was dark and overgrown with weeds. The child tugged at her hand and encouraged her along in its soft wordless voice. She followed hesitantly, searching for points of reference: the tree once split by lightning, the grey livershaped boulder, but she could locate nothing familiar in the web of twisted limbs and matted bark that thickened the darkness. Exhausted and disoriented, she held back. They had gone far from home and were wandering deeper and deeper into the orchard. She could walk no further. Burdock and foxtails heavy with dew tangled around her ankles and the child's fingers now gripping with sinewy strength dug into her sweating palm.

"The swing, there's the swing," she gasped.

The swing rocked under her weight. Overhead fragments of sky blurred into the leafy darkness. The sight made her dizzy. She needed stillness, rest in order to get her bearings. She had always feared dark places: cellars, crevices, hollows. This dark was beyond fear: a damp enclosing blackness into which she and the child – its face opposite her a featureless pallor – had fallen. As the swing continued to sway she began to pray, to plead in choked whispers, "Gentle Jesus, sweet and mild…now I lay me…" bedtime prayers, but the words came out all wrong. "Our Father who are in hell." The voice grew unrecognizable and mocking.

The swing was gaining momentum. Faster and faster it soared, brushing through the branches and when it dropped to skim the ground with uncontrolled speed a spasm stifled her breath. Now it rose even higher to graze the treetops. In those brief moments against the sky she glimpsed the child pumping furiously with its bony arms and legs.

"Reeling wheeling head over heeling" it chanted wildly as the wind swept its hair back from the gaping mouth and the ivory hollows of the eyes and nose.

She reached out and grabbed one arm. A terrible roar exploded in the air. The swing plunged earthward throwing her off balance. She fell, a dry twig in her hand.

A lousy day. Blank. A few squirrels, a rabbit, no deer. He hadn't fired a shot. If only Linda had let John come with him he could have spent the hours teaching the boy how to stay down wind and move noiselessly through the brush. Linda didn't understand. All he wanted was to pass on to his sons what his father had given him. Linda babied them, coddled his mother. Her need to nurture was boundless. She rescued crickets from spider webs, chipmunks from the cat, the cat from the dog, the dog from other dogs. If it were in her power, she would embrace every creature, tame every predator and lull them all into her vision of earthly paradise. A lousy rotten day starting before dawn with his mother screaming and then Linda silently hostile. If John had come with him, he would have drunk water instead of whiskey and now would be headed home instead of squatting in the treehouse drinking more whiskey, watching a blur of clouds and foliage over head, hearing crows and the rattle of dead branches or was it a buck rubbing against a tree trunk. He emptied the flask and dangling his legs over the edge of the platform looked down. Nothing. Wavering light and shadows. The deer path along the stream, empty. He rested his head against the wooden railing, closed his eyes and listened. Insects, his own boozy breathing and then something more, a rustle. He roused himself, picked up his gun and climbed down the ladder shifting his weight slowly from rung to rung. Once on the ground his legs, rubbery with drink, sagged and he needed a moment to get his balance. Then with the loaded gun cradled in his arms he made his way silently on to the deer path.

"What a miserable day," Linda muttered to herself as she stood on the porch. The early morning argument with Rob over his taking John hunting pained her long after he had left the house. The boys sensing her mood had kept out of the way. Now as supper time neared she needed to gather them close. It occurred to her that she hadn't seen Minna for some time.

"Have you seen your grandmother?" she called from the porch.

"Attic." Timmy crouching beside a pile of dead leaves pointed a muddy hand at the roof.

He always answered "attic," a mysterious forbidden place used to store fishing gear and guns.

"She's in the woods," John said and positioned his tank to ram his brother's cannon.

Linda gripped the railing. "She mustn't go there. It's deer season. I can't keep track of all of you every minute of the day and night." At the sight of two bewildered faces she checked herself. "When did you see her go into the woods, John?"

"Don't remember. Will Dad kill a deer?"

The tank rammed the cannon. Timmy started to wail.

"Bring your toys up here and don't move from the porch until I get back."

She stood beside the maple tree at the end of the yard and called for Minna but her voice penetrated no further than the dense thickets of sumac and bayberry and after a backward glance to the children on the porch, she stepped into the woods and searched to orient herself in the maze of trails, but early frost, and autumn winds had transformed the trees, stripping some to tangled skeletons while emblazoning others crimson and gold. She hurried along one path, then another, stopping at forks and then rushing to the left or right until breathless she stopped in a shaded area that looked familiar: a small clearing bordered by a stand of spruce, their bluegreen unchanged by frost. Beyond them would be a path leading to the orchard.

"Minna," she shouted but her cry was obliterated by

an explosion of sound; a shot, a crash followed by a rush of tawny and white bodies stampeding toward her, their great eyes wild with terror. She turned and ran from them fighting her way through tall brush that lashed against her bare arms and face. Protecting her eyes with one hand she plunged ahead hopelessly lost until she heard, "Mom, hurry. Dad's coming."

As she stumbled out of the woods into the yard the boys rushed off the porch.

John yelling "Dad's over there," raced past her.

"Deer, dead deer." Timmy in tears hurled himself against her and buried his face in her skirt.

"Help me with her," Rob called as he walked toward the porch holding the limp body in his arms.

Minna opened her eyes ever so slightly and peeked through the slits. The faded wall paper of roses and ivy was familiar, so were the branches of the locust swaying outside the bedroom window, but she couldn't remember how she came to be in bed. Bits of the past like the pieces in a kaleidoscope came in and out of focus. Faces, four of them, peered at her through the dim bedroom light.

"Don't worry, dears," she said in her mind to them. "No pain. Arms, legs numb, not part of me."

She did remember falling, losing her balance and then being toppled from the swing at the moment a shot rang out and a buck leaped up so close to her she felt the air quiver. The eyes in the faces blinked, small lips blew kisses at her and disappeared leaving the pretty face and beside it an unshaven one. She didn't recall his growing a beard. He had gone away and must have grown it then. She was glad he had come back. She smiled at him and at the pretty face and told them in her mind not to cry but they left the room in tears, holding on to each other.

As soon as they had gone, the child came to the window, dropped from a locust branch to the sill, and cheeping, demanding attention, pressed its pallid face against the screen.

"Go away." She forced the words out from her mind into the air.

It shook its head and waited.

"I've tried to explain it to them but Timmy keeps having nightmares and John does nothing but sulk," Linda told Rob when he came up from the cellar where he had been working all morning without stopping for lunch.

"We should have taken them with us. Seeing her buried would have helped them understand," he said and going to the kitchen sink turned on the tap.

"The weather was bad." She left off ironing one of his shirts and sat down at the kitchen table.

He filled a glass with tap water and looked out the window. "A little rain wouldn't have hurt them. We need lots more. Wood's like tinder."

The porch door was open and from where she sat she could see the faded foliage of oak and wild cherry. The maple stood in a pool of its own fallen leaves, its crest still bright.

"We could take the boys to the cemetery this afternoon when they wake up from their naps," she called down the cellar steps after him.

"Whenever you're ready. I'll be fixing the sump pump or we'll be flooded when it really rains."

As she went back to ironing the sound of metal against metal filled the kitchen. Water glasses on an open shelf vibrated in sympathy. She listened expectantly for the children, awakened suddenly and frightened by the noise, to cry out for her. When no cry came she turned off the iron and went to the bedroom doorway. John lay spread-eagled across the bed, Timmy curled on his side near the edge of the mattress. Resisting the temptation to rearrange him she shut the door quietly.

While Minna had lingered speechless Linda had imposed a rule of silence. No wrestling, voices and the TV kept low. Not a sound in the house but whispers and the murmur of rain. Not a sound in the front bedroom but Minna's shallow breathing and her own choked tears. For three days she had kept the vigil at the bedside, warmed the small, chilled hand in hers, protecting yet clinging to it while Rob and the boys came and went on tip toe. She had let them look after themselves without her. Days and nights had flowed into one endless hour draining her strength. Minna had slipped from her grasp as swiftly and silently as one already drowned, leaving her alone, surrounded by voices.

In the following days noise, loud noise swept through the house in waves. Rob and the boys rushed in and out, up and down playing, working, urging her back to them.

"I've finished," Rob called from the cellar.

"Ready in a minute."

She hurried to the bedroom. Timmy had rearranged himself face down in the center of his bed.

"Did Dad kill a deer?" John, already half awake, asked.

"I've already told you he didn't kill anything. He tripped and when the gun went off, the shot scared the deer."

"What killed Gran?"

"A stroke. She had a stroke and fell off the swing. Now get up so we don't keep your father waiting."

"Where are we going?"

"To visit your grandmother's grave."

She touched Timmy's shoulder gently.

"Me, too," he said lifting his head from the pillow.

A dusty path led to the cemetery on a low treeless hill in the midst of open fields. Linda walked slowly, her eyes half closed against the blazing afternoon sun while in front of her Timmy and John tugged excitedly at their father. As they neared the low stone wall and cast iron gate that enclosed the graves he let go of their hands and shooed them on ahead. They ran kicking up puffs of dust until they reached the gate where they hesitated and looked back.

Rob led the way past rows of small weathered headstones. The bases of some had sunk into the ground; on others the names had worn dim. Pots of red geraniums and yellow chrysanthemums marked the more recent graves but during the summer the plants had grown leggy, the stalks brittle.

"Here." Rob knelt down and removed some stones from the freshly turned soil. Recently seeded, it was still raw and bare. The boys squatted down beside him and then lost interest.

"Let's pick some flowers," Linda said but they were already scampering down the hill to the car.

"You had better go and keep an eye on them. I won't be long," she told Rob.

Clusters of goldenrod and wild asters grew along the wall sheltered from the wind. The sun-baked stone gave off a dry heat. She gathered a small bouquet and stood for a moment by the grave listening to the drowsy hum of insects from the surrounding meadows. The earth was drifting into sleep taking with it the dusty bloom of summer.

The boys went quietly to bed after supper. In the silent evenings preceding Minna's death they had lost the habit of roughhousing and to Linda's relief Rob had made no effort to renew it.

Now as she tucked Timmy in, John bounced up and announced, "Dad's going to take me with him in the woods after school tomorrow."

"Me too." Timmy grabbed her arm. "I'm going to ride in the woods on a hog bush."

"He means a bush hog, Mom." John fell back on the pillow with a sigh.

Linda turned out the light and hurried downstairs. She had seen little of Rob in the ten days since Minna's death. Immediately after the burial service he had thrown himself into repairing farm gates, resetting fence posts, routing out drainage pipes. He ate the meals she left warming on the stove at odd hours. This afternoon after visiting the cemetery with the boys he had disappeared into the cow barn and not returned for supper. Now as she came into the kitchen she saw his plate soaking in the sink and an empty beer can on the table.

"Rob," she called trying to keep her voice calm.

"Out here."

The porch was dark and all she could see was the bulk of his large frame on the wicker bench.

"The boys asleep?"

An arm motioned her toward the bench but she remained standing against the railing, her back to the woods.

"Yes. Did you promise to take them into the woods?"

She looked hard through the shadows for his face, seeing only a white slit of a smile below the dark cavities of his eyes.

"I'm planning to clear the orchard of all that scrub. John can help me with the small stuff. I'll think of something for Timmy."

"And just what is a bush hog?"

He laughed softly. "Don't worry. It's not a wild boar with big tusks. More like a small tractor, it chews up roots, weeds. I'll reopen the old path to the swing. You can relax there and watch us work."

She sat down beside him, folded her hands in her lap and stared in the darkness.

One month ago, Minna had told John and Timmy that the stars were racing faster and faster away from the earth and into outer space. The boys had worried that the sky would soon be empty and in order to get them to sleep Linda had had to explain that their grandmother liked to see things her way. Tonight the sky, a continuous starless dark with the dark woods, looked empty.

"There's rain up there. Low cloud cover and dead air mean lots of rain," Rob said. The wicker bench quivered as he leaned away from her to rest his forearms on his thighs. "We can move back to Clinton if that would make you easier in your mind, more peaceful."

"The country is good for the boys. They can't ride a bush hog with you on Main Street."

"What about you in this house without my mother and with the boys in school?"

"Just hold on to me while I let go," she said and searched the shadows for his hand.

The Pack ✑

"THERE GOES DORA," I said.

Maureen and Nancy joined me at the window to watch Dora still in her long white graduation dress, her arms laden with books, walk away from our dorm. Beside her an older woman carried an open dress carton filled with plaques, framed commendations and books bound in red and green, the school colors, and all the academic prizes Dora had won in her years at Whitfield Hall.

"She can't wait to get away," Nancy said laughing as Dora hurried across the school green to a dusty, two-door sedan.

"She's not the only one," I added quickly, hoping to forestall Maureen from suggesting that maybe we had been too nasty to Dora all these years and most especially with that gross joke of last night.

Maureen was feeling too guilty to be forestalled. "I feel really bad about last night in the tea house. I didn't expect…"

None of us had expected the happening we had

staged in the tea house at Dora's expense to get completely out of control. I didn't want to be reminded of it.

"To hell with Dora. I never want to see her or this shitty place again," Nancy said and the three of us turned from the window to face the mess in my room.

"We won't see her. She's been offered full scholarships at Bryn Mawr, Smith and some other top college," Maureen mused, and picking her way through half-packed suitcases and bulging cartons reached the only chair not covered with clothes.

"She wasn't dumb," Nancy admitted as she examined my new but warped tennis racquet. "You leave this thing out in the rain?"

"Last week. I forgot it."

Nancy sat down on a book carton, I on the unmade bed.

After four years none of us could bring herself to make the first move. Down the hall girls were calling goodbye, shouting phone numbers while in the driveway an impatient parent honked the horn. Suddenly Maureen got to her feet and standing in the middle of the room motioned us to her.

"We must swear to keep together always." Her violet blue eyes filled with tears.

"Always," Nancy and I said in chorus and joining in our three-way hand-over-hand grip swore never to lose touch in the scary world outside "The Hall."

We had hated Whitfield Hall, "a crummy boarding school in the crummy village of Titus, a nowhere spot in crummy Connecticut." Nevertheless, at "The Hall" each of us had achieved a reputation: Nancy the ath-lete with the super "Bod"; Maureen, not too bright, but the prettiest girl in the school; and I was considered the leader. Together the three of us formed our own superior clique known as the Pack, an invincible trio with a talent for nastiness.

For three of our four years the focus of our malice had been Dora Caswell. A lumpy, awkward girl on a scholarship, she had joined our class in the second year, by which time cliques had been formed and the Pack had consolidated its dominant position. Bewildered and friendless, she was a natural target. Too shy to try for the drama or other clubs, too clumsy to be a good ath-lete, she fell back on her one endowment: brains. A straight A student in all subjects, she was not above patronizing lesser lights with "That test wasn't bad."

We set the tone with "So what. She's a grind. She has to get As. She's on a scholarship."

One term, Nancy stole her lab notes before the sci-ence exam. I disrupted her oral report on Keats by mut-tering from *The Eve of St. Agnes*,

And now, my love, my seraph fair, awake!
Thou art my heaven, and I thine eremite.

which set the entire class sniggering.

Dora never struck back. On the contrary, she seemed ever present, ever anxious to please with, "You can bor-row my notes anytime. Nancy should be captain of the varsity."

At first we were flattered by her admiration. Timid and lonely outside the classroom, she wanted to be like us, to share our self-confidence, our indifference to school rules. Perhaps she thought that as a member of the Pack she could join us in finding new victims. In time, however, her fawning disgusted us and I suspect that her admiration turned to envy and finally hate, although we had no inkling of the change. She continued to haunt our every move. Overhearing some jibe of mine, she would tilt her head and smile. She regularly scrutinized Nancy's grace on the basketball court with her pale grey eyes.

"I feel like puking when she turns those eyes on me," Nancy complained.

"Don't be dumb. It's like the rabbit and the snake. You're the snake."

"And she's no innocent little rabbit. She's a tattle tale and a snitch," Nancy snapped.

Even Maureen, who occasionally felt sorry for Dora agreed that although we had no proof, Dora must have reported my cache of pot hidden in a Noxema jar and Nancy's scotch in a Listerine bottle.

"Sure, her way of sucking up to the powers that be," Nancy concluded.

Maureen wrinkled her beautiful brow and said cautiously, "I guess maybe Dora isn't a good person."

"She's a rotten person," I said, laughing at Maureen's innocence.

We all agreed and felt encouraged to plan our next move.

In our senior year Dora received less of our attention. Now boys dominated our every waking moment. In an obsessive haze we thought, talked, fantasized boys. A new sports car parked on campus, a popular song on the radio triggered images of handsome profiles, windblown hair and athletic bodies. By the middle of the spring term these visions had acquired names. Maureen was practically engaged to Frank Wilson, Nancy was madly in love with Tom Cowles and I spent hours on the phone with Chris Hamilton. As the weather grew warmer, the days longer and the campus lawns bloomed white and yellow with spring flowers, the Pack's ecstatic mood centered on the senior dance. This was always held the night before graduation. It would be the Pack's last chance to shine, to leave its mark forever in the annals of Whitfield Hall. But how? In the sunny afternoons of April we gathered to deliberate. Our favorite meeting place was a small Victorian tea house on the campus grounds, a charming remnant of the days when Whitfield Hall had been a private estate. Constructed of wood, with sides of white lattice, it was just large enough for the three of us and stood hidden in a grove of ancient lilacs at the end of a path lined with privet. There we discussed the dance: what would we wear, what time would the boys arrive from New Haven, had we got the best room in the dorm set aside for guests? But the principal question remained unanswered and graduation was less than a month away. Unless we thought of something soon the Pack's days of glory would end in a whimper.

One evening while waiting for Nancy and Maureen, I stood at the window in search of inspiration. On the campus, below the globes of the street lamps hung glazed in mist and barely visible in the distance, the pointed roof of the little tea house rose through the leafy darkness.

"Hey, come here and listen to this," Nancy said coming into the room. "Maureen says that Frank told her that his cousin Charlie's sister has just split with Gregg."

We had heard plenty about the jock, the stallion of Titus. I had suspected that Frank might be using these accounts of his cousin's sister's alleged exploits as a means to proposition the chaste Maureen. Nancy and I warned her unnecessarily. She was afraid of real sex. We all were, and while the notorious Gregg, seducer and sexual athlete figured in our fevered fantasies, he had no place in our world. Gregg was from Titus, he went to some community college and, it was said, worked in his father's garage. Such boys called us "Whitfield Haulers." To us they were simply "Townies" and no girl from the Hall would have anything to do with them. It was precisely Gregg's combination of social leper and local libertine that made me envisage him as suitable for our last and greatest feat.

I led the way to Dora's room. We found her alone and half asleep at her desk. Under questioning she admitted she had been too busy studying to have given any thought to the dance. Maureen, whose prettiness always gave an impression of innocence, explained that there was this neat guy, a friend of her boyfriend's cousin, who'd love to be invited. Dora listened, scrutinized Maureen's delicate features, Nancy's slender limbs and then stared at me.

"Com'on, Dora," I urged. "You'd be doing him a favor. Some bitch has just walked out on him."

Gregg's loneliness struck the right chord and in the days that followed an invitation was sent to Gregg with Frank acting as go-between. To our relief it was accepted. Then we took Dora in hand. She responded in her stolid way, joined us at Armand's Beauty Salon, bought make-up at the local drugstore and under my guidance came to Hartford where she spent most of her savings from a summer job on an evening dress of pale coral chiffon with a long pleated skirt, full enough to hide her lumpy figure, and a bodice trimmed with tiny pearls and gold beads.

"She still looks pretty pathetic," I reported to Maureen.

"Even in that super dress? Never mind. I'll help her fix her hair and with make-up to cover the spots she'll pass."

Frank had been instructed to tell his cousin Charlie to brief Gregg about his Whitfield Hall date. "Shy, cool on the surface but with the right guy a real swinger. Dumps men like they were spent rockets, dances like a dervish." Word came back that all Gregg's systems were "go."

The weather the night of the dance was perfect, the air so warm and still that the sides of the big green and white tent could be rolled up and tables set around it on the grass. Our dates arrived together from Yale and we rushed across the lawn to meet them. My Chris looked divine in a white dinner jacket. Frank brought Maureen a pale pink carnation to match his boutonniere. She wore it in her hair which she had rinsed that afternoon with Emberglo so that it shone with fascinating blue black highlights. Tom gazed admiringly at Nancy, suntanned and svelte in white lace. We stood chatting under the trees. Out of the corner of my eye I could see Dora standing alone watching us.

"Ask Frank where's the stud," I whispered anxiously to Chris.

"Relax. He'll show."

"Probably gone to pick up a tux at the rental place," Tom suggested.

"I can't wait to see him," Nancy giggled.

The music started and as couples began to move into the tent the Pack became nervous.

"I'm afraid Dora'll panic," I said.

Frank who had met Gregg once with Charlie's sister was elected to go look for him in the parking lot and I motioned to Dora to join us. The music had picked up tempo and Nancy and Tom were grappling with each other, dancing a version of the Sidewinder on the grass while the rest of us hummed and clapped. Dora was starting to sweat. Her blonde hair was wet at the hairline and the long chiffon sleeves clung damply to her arms.

"I think I'll go to the john," she whined.

"No, wait here." I grabbed her hand. "He'll come."

He came, all six foot three in a black ill fitting tuxedo, dwarfing Frank and strolling along with his hands in his pockets, real cool, not hurrying towards us. His hair, dark and curly, was combed straight back and he wore smoke tinted glasses that accentuated the paleness of his face.

Seeing him Nancy broke off dancing with Tom and rushed over to me. "Wow, the Black Stallion," she whispered breathlessly.

Maureen pulled Dora forward with her.

"Hello, Gregg, I'm Maureen and this is Dora."

The rest of us closed in around them. Gregg nodded silently at the introductions. Dora fumbled with her evening purse.

"We're all at table one," Nancy said nervously. "Come when you get thirsty. The punch isn't much good but…."

Gregg looked over the top of her head and then turning to Dora said, "Let's dance."

As they disappeared into the tent, the Pack exchanged looks of disappointment. In terms of our expectations the meeting had bombed. No signs of outrage, no quivers of lust on Gregg's part, and Dora had been her usual drippy self.

By the time Chris and I reached the dance floor it was crowded. We clung to each other with self-absorbed determination, joining the Pack for punch when the band took a break. From time to time we caught glimpses of Dora and Gregg – a brief passage of coral chiffon and black polyester soon lost in the flow of bodies. When the music stopped they drifted out of sight into the semi-darkness of the campus grounds.

After one intermission they were among the first to return to the dance floor.

"He's sure good," Nancy observed. "That's real break dancing." The band accelerated the beat and Gregg whirling and bobbing took over the center of the floor. The crowd began to clap and formed a circle around him, blocking our view.

"Let's go watch." Maureen got up from her chair.

"No," I said firmly. "Look at the time."

It was ten minutes to midnight. When the clock in the chapel tower struck the hour the band would play "Good Night Ladies."

"She's right," Chris said checking his watch. "Now remember. Wait for my signal. Don't rush it."

We left the table, each couple taking a separate route into the darkness.

I clutched Chris' hand and hampered by my long dress struggled to keep up with him. The grass under the trees was damp and slippery and soon my evening shoes were soaked. The sound of the music grew fainter.

"How are we doing?" I asked excitedly as he released my hand to look at his watch.

"Right on schedule. Come on."

"You're sure Gregg knows where?"

"He knows."

I hurried along at his side, worrying in silence. If anything went wrong the Pack would blame me. The scheme had been my idea. We skirted the rows of privet and headed for a clump of overgrown forsythia. Crouching behind it, we waited tensely. Through the tangle of branches we could make out the tea house. It stood isolated and silent in its shelter of lilacs. The last faint strokes of the chapel clock died in the trees. The music had stopped and the still night air seemed to close in on us. I felt Chris' hand tighten around mine. A mixture of muffled sounds: a deep voice, footsteps, creaking boards broke the stillness. We crept forward, staying low in the shadows and cautiously working our way into the lilac bushes. The noise of a scuffle came from inside the tea house and through the narrow slits of the lattice I could see the glint of beads and flutter of chiffon. Beside me Chris was slowly raising his arm. A branch snapped against his shoulder. A whine filled the tea house and then I heard a click. Suddenly the interior of the building was drenched in light. Jeering we rushed out of the bushes and with the Pack behind us dashed around to the entrance. Dora lay squirming on the wooden floor half hidden under Gregg who was struggling to disentangle himself from the layers of her skirt. As he got to his feet his dark glasses skittered across the boards. He faced us, his enormous physique and pallid features rigid with anger. Then he turned away and zipped up his fly. On a signal from Chris, Tom switched off the light and as we ran away we could hear Dora whimpering in the darkness.

At graduation the next day she appeared red-eyed and sullen. Word of the Pack's farewell coup had spread through the school. As a result each time she went to the dais to receive all Whitfield Hall's important academic prizes she had to run the gauntlet of curious glances, whispers and sly laughter that accompanied the applause. The Pack clapped loudest of all but she ignored us and immediately after the ceremony drove away with her parents and out of our lives and thoughts.

Upon leaving Whitfield Hall the Pack dispersed. College, travel, jobs intervened. Nevertheless we kept in touch and in time as the boyfriends became husbands we attended each other's weddings. Chris, Frank and Tom went to work in Hartford and as a consequence we found ourselves all living in Eastwood, a new housing development midway between Titus and Hartford. The houses were flimsy structures with picture windows and numerous shutters and bits of wrought iron to give them a customized appearance. However, they fit our budgets as young marrieds. Our husbands car pooled to work. Maureen, Nancy and I shopped for bargains, made curtains and exchanged recipes. Every Friday night we got together after dinner at one of our houses to play poker, a penny ante game that usually broke up around eleven.

One winter evening Frank remarked that he had run into Gregg Stockton while waiting for a bus in Hartford. They had talked briefly. Gregg, it seemed, was doing well. He had taken over his father's garage in Titus and expanded into the retailing of auto parts.

"The guy's a hustler. He's got several stores in Norwalk and Bridgeport. Must be leveraged up to his eyes."

"Who isn't?" Tom added somewhat grimly.

At the mention of Gregg Stockton, Maureen, Nancy and I laughed recalling the scene in the tea house.

"We were awful at school," I said. "Poor Dora."

"Poor Dora was an envious little snitch, a born informer," Nancy said.

"Never see her name in the alumnae bulletin. I wonder what happened to her," Maureen mused.

"Married Gregg," Frank said. "Now let's play poker."

"Married Gregg!" the Pack cried in one voice. "When? Where are they living?"

He hadn't bothered to ask.

"You guys go ahead and play," I said as Maureen, Nancy and I gathered on the sofa at the other end of the living room to consult the phone book.

"Here it is. G. Stockton Jr. 10 Center Street, Titus."

For a moment we sat silently around the coffee table.

"I feel a plot in the making." Nancy laughed pointing at me. "Just like old times."

"No plot but I do think it would be interesting to see the charming couple. Maybe they play poker."

"If he's such a whiz at business, he's probably a terrific poker player."

"He sure could dance," Maureen added irrelevantly.

I picked up the phone and dialed the number. Dora answered in her familiar monotone. In the background a hi-fi was playing classical music. I explained that Nancy, Maureen and I had recently moved to Eastwood with our husbands and Frank had enjoyed bumping into Gregg and we should all get together one evening.

Dora was non-committal. She'd have to ask her husband when he came home. He was very busy. Yes, they enjoyed cards, especially bridge.

"How about poker? Next Friday at my house?"

"Gregory likes to gamble. I'll let you know tomorrow," she replied and hung up.

I did not hear from her the next day, Saturday or on the subsequent Sunday or Monday. On Tuesday Maureen, Nancy and I met for lunch in the Eastwood mall cafeteria prior to checking out the linen sales.

"God, I loathe this place," Nancy grumbled as we sat down with our trays of salad and coffee. "It reminds me of boarding school, speaking of which, what about Dora?"

"Haven't heard a word."

We couldn't agree on a next move. To call her again would be demeaning. Obviously the girl had no manners, a born loser and that townie husband....

Maureen, who was five months pregnant and growing more doe-eyed and saccharine by the day, wondered if maybe Dora didn't have a right to bear a grudge after the grief the Pack had inflicted on her at Whitfield Hall.

"That was years ago," I snapped. "I'm sure she's forgotten all about those silly jokes. She was perfectly pleasant on the phone. I'll phone her tomorrow morning. Now let's shop."

That same evening as Chris and I were sitting down to dinner the phone rang.

"This is Gregory Stockton," a bass baritone voice said.

Startled to hear from him rather than from Dora I rattled on with "love to see you both, hope you can come, just a fun game of poker."

"We'll be there," he said.

Friday evening we gathered promptly at my house to await the arrival of the Stocktons. We always played at one end of the living room – "the dining alcove" in the words of the developer – and as I was covering the table and putting out the chips I noticed that everyone was standing around the picture window at the other end of the room.

"Hey. Don't be so crass. If we can see them, they can see us," I cautioned.

"That must be them now," Frank said, "in the BMW wagon."

"Great car," Chris mused.

"Probably got it cheap. He's in the business."

I went to the peephole in the front door.

"How does she look?" Nancy hovering behind me asked.

"It's too dark to see much except that he's taller than ever. Here they come. Act casual everybody."

The bell rang and I opened the door.

"Come in out of the cold you two," I said cheerily. "Chris will take your coats."

Gregg wasn't wearing an overcoat.

"He doesn't mind the cold," Dora said handing Chris her fur jacket. Ranch mink, the Pack's glances noted.

They came into the living room and stood side by side while we made conversation. However, the men soon found the common topic of cars, leaving Maureen, Nancy and me to talk at Dora. She was still rather dumpy, wore no make-up but her complexion had cleared and the limp blonde hair was improved by a feather cut. As in the past, the grey eyes scrutinized each of us but now more confidently.

"When's the baby due?" she asked Maureen.

"In May. Have you any children?"

I foresaw a tiresome dialogue – breast feeding, Montessori, toilet training – but Dora's blunt "No" killed it.

"You and Maureen get the men to the table," I said hurriedly. "Nancy and I will bring the coffee."

"No coffee for us," Dora said.

Once in the kitchen Nancy exploded.

"There's something about that girl that makes me want to gouge out her eyes."

I agreed that Dora's stare still stirred the sadistic impulses.

Gregg's deep voice reached us from the living room.

"Five-card stud. Ten dollar ante. No limit on raises."

"My God," Nancy gasped. "Those are crazy stakes. Didn't you make clear we just play a social game?"

"Of course I did. Don't panic. I'm sure our husbands will cope."

"You underestimate the male ego," Nancy muttered and followed me into the next room.

Chris was seated at one end of the table, Gregg at the other. He had removed his jacket and loosened his tie. With his long waisted muscular torso and broad shoulders he looked cramped, but while waiting for Nancy and me to take our places, he sat quietly with his hands folded on the green felt, large hands with prominent knuckles. I noticed that the fingernails had been bitten down to the quick.

"I prefer to watch," Dora announced and pulled her chair well away from the table.

Although she positioned it to insure that she could not see Gregg's or anyone else's hand, she annoyed me, sitting stiffly with Gregg's jacket folded across her lap, his black attaché case on the floor at her feet.

Chris, avoiding my eyes, explained the stakes: One hundred dollar limit, three raises; a compromise from those proposed by Gregg. Tom and Frank nodded. Maureen and Nancy looked at me despairingly but before I could protest the men had already anted ten dollars apiece. We played grudgingly, defensively, the more so because our husbands, obviously enjoying the challenge, were raising and calling recklessly. Between rounds they quipped among themselves with the forced jocularity of friends in the presence of a stranger. Gregg ignored all of us. He stacked his chips in silence while Dora sat immobile and expressionless as if waiting for the evening to end.

After an hour no one had won or lost a significant amount. Then Gregg began to win, primarily at Chris' expense. He played methodically and consistently well and in time his fierce concentration communicated itself to the rest of us. The joking ceased. The cards dropped as silently as feathers on the green felt and with inexorable regularity Gregg's large hand drew the chips from the center of the table. The Pack was no match for him.

At the end of a hand I heard Dora ask, "May I get a glass of water?"

"Sure. Let's take a break." Chris got up from his chair. "Who wants a drink? Whiskey, brandy, white wine?"

"Just water," Dora said.

He handed her a glass of Perrier and then asked, "What about you, Gregg?"

"Brought my own. Where's my attaché case, Hon?"

Dora gave it to him and the Pack watched with fascination as he opened it on the floor and took out a bottle of cheap blended whiskey.

Drinks in hand we returned to the table. As I dealt I was conscious of Dora's eyes fixed on me. Her presence, the sound of the water fizzing in her glass, Gregg's bulk at the end of the table, the grim tenor of the competition depressed me and I prayed that Chris would recoup some of his losses so that we could all quit with good grace. He did win the hand and the next one. Soon the pressure of winning replaced that of losing. Now it became the Pack against Gregg with Chris in the lead and growing increasingly aggressive. I began to feel uneasy. The game had lost any semblance of sociability and the men were drinking and gambling hard. When Maureen, looking pale and strained, excused herself, Nancy and I left the table as well.

"I'm sorry," I said as the three of us settled on the sofa at the far end of the living room. "It was meant to be amusing."

"A long evening, that's for sure." Nancy yawned. "I just hope Tom quits when he's ahead."

"Frank's drinking too much," Maureen added wearily.

Numb with fatigue and boredom we waited listening to ice rattling in glasses, the click of chips and the slurred voices of our husbands. Gregg spoke only to bet and his tone never varied. Dora remained in her chair.

"Why the hell is she staring at us," Nancy grumbled and folded her long legs under her.

I reminded her that Dora had always done that. "Couldn't keep her eyes off the Pack."

"Sure, the rabbit and the snake."

"Maybe she'd like to sit here with us," Maureen suggested. "Shall I go ask her?"

"Don't. We're miserable enough as it is. Besides since I'm the hostess of this gruesome event, I'm going to stop that game at twelve o'clock. You be ready to back me up. Tell Frank you want to go home. A pregnant woman's right to leave at midnight."

Maureen smiled wanly and crossed her hands over her stomach. I rested my head on the back of the sofa and watched the snow drifting past the picture window. Large wet flakes floated through the light and then sank into the darkness. The roads would be slippery and neither Frank nor Tom in any condition to drive. I worried about Maureen. Nancy would have to take them home. Suddenly I heard someone shouting. Gregg was coming toward us, clapping his hands.

"Midnight. Everybody line up," he yelled.

"What the hell is going on?" Frank yelled back weaving up to him. "You a bad loser or someth'n? A lousy five hundred dollars."

"Frank, please," Maureen pleaded.

"Com' on girls, over there against the wall, next to your husbands," Gregg ordered.

"Sounds like an execution." Tom emptied his glass.

"Maybe he wants to take our picture." Maureen struggled out of the sofa.

"Yeah," Gregg laughed loudly. "Theodora wants a picture of the Pack."

Nancy and I followed Maureen across the room to where Tom and Chris stood looking bleary-eyed and bewildered. Frank had slumped into an armchair and was about to fall asleep.

Gregg, his face flushed, his big hands clenched, glared down at him for a moment and then bellowed, "Up!"

Chris and Tom started for Gregg but Frank opened his eyes, motioned them back and got to his feet. He shuffled over to us.

"There you see it, Hon." Gregg drew Dora to his side. "The Whitfield Pack."

"The Pack," she echoed taking us in one by one.

"Look here, Gregg," Chris called over to him. "Enough games. Let's have a drink and then everyone can go home."

"You've had enough already, Yaley," Gregg snarled. "We're leaving but don't anybody move. Get your coat, Theodora."

He stood, hands on his hips, scowling at us while Dora went to the closet.

I could make no sense of the scene: Gregg and Dora, acting as if they had rehearsed every move, playing king of the castle in my living room, she in her mink jacket, the expression on her face suddenly animated, expectant, her eyes alert while we stood dazed, our husbands boozey, bunched together like cattle in a storm.

Maureen had started to cry quietly. In a fury I broke away and walked up to Dora.

"Damn it. Can't you see she's…."

Gregg stepped between us, his huge body blocking me.

"Get back in the Pack where you belong." He raised his hand as if about to push me.

As I stepped aside Chris rushed over. "You rotten Townie." He struck out wildly with his fist.

Gregg caught him by the wrist and shoved him back against the wall.

"Townie, Titus Townie bastard," Frank mumbled. "Play dirty, fight dirty."

"You'd all better do what Gregory wants," Dora said tensely.

"What the hell is that, Gregg?"

"Strip."

Nobody moved. We stared at them, they at us immobilized by mutual loathing.

"Strip," Gregg shouted and slapped his thigh.

The Pack huddled closer. "The guy's psycho. Keep cool. But he's dangerous. No, just bombed. You grab Dora. I'll call the police. Wait. Look out. He's got a gun."

"Gregory does have a gun." Dora pointed to the bulging pocket of his jacket.

We stripped and clung husband and wife while Gregg paced back and forth, his right hand in his pocket.

"O.K. Theodora. There's your picture. The Pack. Look, damn it." With his left hand he pushed her toward us. "Where's all that great stuff you keep telling me about? Beautiful Maureen – just a big belly with blue veins. And the other two, the Bod and the Brain – Nothin'. They've got nothin'."

Dora's grey eyes now alive with rage searched us, darting avidly across our nakedness, probing our bodies. Gregg's language grew more violent and obscene. He was baiting her as well as us.

"Look at your Whitfield Haulers and their fuckin' New Haven hubbies. A bunch of shit."

Dora began to tremble. Her shoulders, first one, then the other twitched. She pressed her arms rigidly to her sides in an effort to gain control but her face seemed to come apart, each feature working, sagging, quivering. Big round tear drops rolled down her cheeks and disappeared in the glossy fur of her jacket.

"Yes," she said in a dull voice. "They're nothing. Let's go home."

On his way out Gregg stopped and flipped the light switch. We waited in the darkness until we heard the front door slam.

The next morning I pretended to be asleep until I heard Chris leave the house. Then I got up and passing through the living room noticed Gregg's black attaché case under the chair Dora had occupied. I placed it on the dining room table, still cluttered with poker chips, ash trays and glasses, and opened it. The bottle of whiskey was nearly full. He and Dora had staged the entire evening: the stakes, his winning, then losing. The Pack had been expertly set up. As I put the bottle back in the attaché case I noticed a leather wallet with the initials G.S. stamped in gold. It contained snapshots. Dora in her wedding dress, a short dress with a modest white veil. Dora under a palm tree (honeymoon?). Dora on a bicycle (Bermuda?). Picture after picture of her smiling, waving, mugging joyfully at the camera.

Later that morning I made a parcel of the attaché case and its contents and took it to the post office.

During the next several days the snow continued to fall intermittently. Then a thaw followed by a freeze left the roads especially hazardous at night. We postponed our poker game to the following week but Chris had to go out of town unexpectedly so it was cancelled again. The following month Nancy and Tom came down with colds; I went to visit my mother in Greenwich and none of us seemed to find the time to press for a resumption of our weekly meeting. In May Maureen gave birth to a baby girl and the Pack gathered to celebrate at a christening party. We embraced, drank lots of champagne, toasted the newborn noisily and on parting promised to get together every Friday evening. Chris would get out the barbecue, Nancy would make the salad, Maureen could bring the baby, but we all knew it would never happen.

The Baby Grand 🎶

IN THE LIVING ROOM your beloved baby grand is mute. Its varnished surface still shines unblemished above my old hiding place, a haven for shadows, but by now the baby's guts probably need tuning. I wouldn't know since you didn't pass along to me the perfect pitch gene. Let's face it. What I got I got from him who – *fortissimo* – left you me and a framed photo of himself on the piano in the living room that your students and musical friends thought had such superb acoustics. They're still terrific. Your every breath carries. No silence falls unheard in this dying room.

You gave up on me early, wasted no lullabies at the bedside of a tone deaf dud of a son. You sang Schubert, Brahms and from under the piano – *adagio adagio* – I spied on the loafers and patent leather pumps of song loving guys who stilled the *lieder* on your lips – *langsam* – broken chords, sighs, a kiss – *sehr langsam* – slipped my way as your hands abandoned the keys.

Your hands in your lap, wrists cocked like a mannequin's, appear detached from the blanketed rest, hunched in a wheelchair.

"Does the new medicine help?" I ask playing straight man to whatever mood you choose.

On good days you lash out vigorously, "I'm ready for dispatch. Send me Express to Elsewhere."

Today from some cavity behind the eyes you lie, "I'm better," and drum thin fingers on the arms of the chair.

Drum Schubert, Brahms? I wonder.

"Bach for Christmas," you said every December: oratorios, psalms when I wanted "Deck the Halls" and the piano piled with presents.

Oh holy night, Oh mother and son.

In spring you sang arias. Your fingers darted like caged finches. *Bel canto* in ascent filled this room with moonlight. Pale lovers and nightingales routed my Rock Pop stomping heroes to oblivion and at song's end you bowed your head, savored the last vibrations in your hands and wept. *O amor, perduto incanto.*

At dusk the grand's luster dulls. It revives when I light the lamp beside your wheelchair. Under the green shade incandescent filaments hum sounds of summer.

"Absurd," you say. "Locusts in late November."

The light wavers. Its skewed rays fall on the nest of faded flowers and dead fledglings in your lap. You scrutinize me and rage silently in the bone place behind your eyes.

I vaguely remember Schubert died young, Brahms at a fine age and Bach's sons played for him.

Peak ໃ

HE HAD STRUCK HER, just one slap to the side of
the face years ago when during a petty argument she
had rushed at him, a small creature flailing the space
between them like a toy robot out of control. By chance
his hand had met her cheek when he had raised it to
ward off her fists.

"I'm leaving you and your bad temper, Ed Hall," she
had cried and taken the two little boys with her, but
two days later she had returned to the mobile home
saying, "It was an accident. We love each other."

He had wrapped his long arms around the three of
them until the children wriggled away leaving him free
to show how tenderly he loved her. They agreed to forget the accident, never to let their tempers get the better of them and to live happily ever after. During subsequent arguments – she objected to his working nights,
he liked the graveyard shift and refused to change – he
had let her do the pacing and door slamming while he
stood, fists clenched deep in his pockets.

Over the years the effort of self-control soured the

passionate sweetness of the reconciliations, left him chronically edgy and now as he stood in the living room about to go to work, the blare of the TV infuriated him.

"I can't sleep in this place. When I'm home I need silence. No TV, no radio, no stereo," he shouted at the two males slouched in front of the screen. They roused themselves and went out the front door.

"Don't you ever raise your hand to them," she shouted back from across the room, and with a sweep of her small hand and the pitch of her voice informed everyone in the Paradise Valley Trailer Park that he, Ed Howard, the Wild World theme park security guard who carried a night stick as thick as your wrist, was an irascible husband and father, unfit for humankind. When the tiny scar on her cheekbone reddened he looked at his hands, the ridges of knuckles and deltas of blue veins. In high school the coach had encouraged him to go in for boxing, saying, "With your mitts and long reach you'll be real good." Upon discovering the punishing power of his fists against a punching bag he had quit in favor of track. Since that one accident with her years ago he kept his distance, never lifted so much as a finger against anyone, least of all against their sons whom she now protected so loudly.

"You've got nothing to be afraid of," he said and slammed the door. It closed and then sprang open releasing a shaft of TV light and noise that trailed him into the darkness.

From the steel and glass booth at the entrance to the Wild World park he was able to keep watch on the parking lot and the chain link fence that protected it from the highway. The lot was deserted at this hour except for a few staff cars basking in the amber glow of flood lights. After placing his thermos and lunch box on the shelf next to the clock he left the booth and walked back and forth inside the barrier gate to work off his pent-up anger. At the far end of the lot rusticated posts topped by barbed wire marked the boundary of the park's three hundred acres. A few poplars pushed by the wind leaned over the fence into the light and then sank back into the darkness that enveloped the animal habitats. From within the enclosure a cry rose, the voice of some nocturnal creature. He halted outside the booth and looking up met a host of eyes. Monkeys, deers, cats huddled together and peered out of a gaudy jungle and higher still in a cutout above their tawny heads a dolphin arched its silver blue body and grinned. "Thrill to life in the wild. Hundreds of exotic birds, beasts. See Winnie, the star of the dancing dolphins perform incredible stunts," the illuminated billboard promised. He retreated inside the booth and shut the door against Winnie's smile. The boys who worked for the park kept urging him to come and see her but he refused ever to set foot inside the enclosure.

"Come on, Dad. Winnie likes doing tricks," they insisted, their mother adding, "That animal is better off than you, a man six foot three closed in a steel box no bigger than a coffin."

He sat down on the stool and poured a cup of coffee from his thermos. Suddenly light from the highway filled the booth. As the blurred line of chrome and single headlights raced by, one of the helmeted riders waved a gloved hand.

The remaining hours of the night passed quietly. He ate in slow stages, finished the coffee and watched for signs of morning. Traffic on the highway increased and the white stripes on the asphalt of the parking lot became visible.

The booth door opened.

"Sorry I'm late, Ed. Damned car wouldn't start." Joe Hamill squeezed his way in. "I know your ever loving gets riled if you're not home on time for breakfast."

"No problem, Joe. I'm not going home. Do me a favor and tell the office I won't be back for a while."

"How come? You sick?"

"No, but I've got plenty of sick leave due me."

The log cabin was chilly in the early morning. He sat in the open doorway waiting for the warmth of sunshine still trapped in the treetops to reach him. The woods were quiet except for the distant shriek of a hawk that circled overhead before riding the thermals southward. Wild shrubs edged the clearing in front of the cabin, the dense gray-green brightened here and there by crimson bayberry and sumac, but it was the silent passage of silver behind the screen of foliage that caught his attention. He remained motionless. The silver took on a touch of white, then a dark stripe that came to a point above the eyes. He met the stare before it withdrew into the shadows.

She returned each morning, a young she wolf with a magnificent grey and black coat and a blaze of white across the chest. He called her Peak because of the dark line like a widow's peak on her brow. Shy at first, she kept to the edge of the clearing, watching him over one shoulder while he went about his chores. Then she grew bolder and followed at a distance as he hurried through the woods to check the posted signs. The woods were full of deer, pheasant and other game and although the cabin and his land were well hidden at the end of an abandoned logging road and surrounded by a large tract protected by the nature conservancy, each fall he discovered the remains of camp fires and signs torn down. For now, the signs were undisturbed but when he headed back to the cabin along a deer path he came upon spent shells behind an outcropping of rock. He kicked them into a pile. As he bent over to collect them she grew curious and circled closer, scenting the air.

"Take a good sniff, Peak." He held out a cartridge. "Remember this. It's bad stuff."

She licked his hand and then ran off.

Her trust worried him.

"Leave the wild ones be. Fear is their only protection," his father had warned him when as a boy he had wanted to adopt every fledgling and litter of orphaned fox kits.

He let her be, tried to ignore her when he saw her waiting for him. Yet while he caulked windows and repaired weather stripping to make the cabin tight for winter he was continually aware of an alert but silent presence nearby. Sometimes she drowsed in the tall grass and merely opened her eyes wide in answer to his "had a good night's hunting, Peak?" More often she was playful. The plastic pail at the water pump could be nosed over and made to roll. Chipmunks and mice hid in the wood pile. After a couple of hours he would take a break, look around and find her gone.

One afternoon while he was working on the cabin roof he glimpsed her running with her kind, five of them in single file behind a large male. It was the only time he ever saw them but at night he would hear first one, then a second, until the entire pack joined. Wide awake, he got out of bed and stood shivering in the clearing. After the silence of his days the swelling chorus drew him in, carried him far into the tree layered darkness. The rhythm quickened, slowed as the voices merged to the pulsing cry of a siren. A young voice more highly pitched than the others rose and he answered "Peak Peak" in long phrases that left him breathless. A few scattered notes replied and the music ceased. Then he returned to bed and slept.

The warmth of autumn cooled. Peak's coat darkened. Whenever she brushed against his leg, he felt its thickness. With work on the cabin completed he was free to sit in the doorway, the heat from the wood stove at his back, the cold air in his face as he watched her watch chickadees and cardinals peck at balls of suet he had hung in a nearby birch.

One frosty morning after a night of high winds he went into the woods to collect fallen branches for kindling. She trotted beside him. On the way back to the cabin a stick of wild cherry fell from the bundle. She pounced, picked it up and crouched facing him. He took it from her and threw it. She retrieved it.

Thereafter, the game became part of her daily visit although he was reluctant to indulge her. Whenever he refused to play, grumbling "You're no bird dog," she would worry the stick and brush against him until he gave in.

One day the wild cherry broke in half. He trimmed the sharp twigs off an aspen branch. She sniffed the unfamiliar wood but at the toss bounded out of the clearing after it.

"Hello, Dad."

He turned to see the boys on the logging road.

"Jim Jensen from the park is with us," one of them said.

Jensen, a heavy set man with "Wild World" stitched on the pocket of his coverall stepped forward.

"Hi, Ed. Great camp you've got here. Your boys have told me all about it."

"You two been spying on me?"

"Mom sent us to find out if you were okay. From the road we could see you were always busy so we left."

"I'm still busy." The sumac behind him rustled faintly.

"I'd sure like to see your tame wolf," Jensen said.

"She's not tame."

"Wolves are big with the public these days. The boys tell me she does tricks. We could use her at the park and pay you a finder's fee."

"She's not for sale and you're trespassing!" he yelled at the three burly figures. He hadn't spoken except to

Peak for weeks. The sound and rage of old arguments surged with tremendous force. "Get going."

The boys stepped back when he raised his hand toward the road but Jensen held his ground.

"Cool it, Ed. You sure have a short fuse. The animals in Wild World are well cared for, protected from predators and leg traps that let the likes of her bleed to death. Think it over and if you don't want the fee the boys will collect it. Those motorcycles eat money." Jensen held out his hand. "How about it?"

"Come back tomorrow. I'm busy mornings. Come at noon."

After they disappeared around the bend in the road he went to the edge of the woods. The stick lay where it had landed in a tangle of wild grape. He retrieved it and went into the cabin.

The dawn air was frigid, the ground white with frost. He got up earlier than usual, a change of routine that must have made her wary because there was no sign of her. He waited in the center of the clearing and when she didn't appear he waved the stick and called, "Peak, come here, Peak."

She emerged from the thicket and stood, head cocked, weight poised on her hind quarters.

The stick whirled through the air, at times landing upended and springing out of sight. He threw it farther and farther. Each time she returned and dropped it in his hand.

"Game's over," he said finally but she looked up at him, panting, ready for more.

"Okay. One last time." He pointed to a distant spruce

and when she turned her head in anticipation of the throw, he brought the stick straight down. The wood shattered across her withers and sent splinters into his palm. He let go of the stub and watched as the sumac settled silently into the mesh of underbrush.

Jensen followed by the boys walked into the clearing. "That's one hell of a road, Ed. I had to back the truck in."

"I'll asphalt it over for you," he said and continued to stack newly split logs onto the wood pile.

"Cabin sure looks snug." Jensen peered into the open doorway.

"When we were little kids we used to come here for the Christmas tree. Right, Dad?"

"Right," he said, but the two bearded faces in no way matched his memory of pink cheeks and tongues licking snow off bright red lips.

"Hal Walker at the park will look after your wolf. He's a good man," Jensen said.

"She's not mine."

"I've got a cage in the truck, one of those humane traps, but you'll have to set it. She knows your scent. I'm told she comes when you call. What's her name?"

"Peak, right, Dad?"

His lungs ached against his ribs as he held his breath.

"Great name, Peak." Jensen shaded his eyes and looked into the woods. "The public will love it."

"She won't come," he said keeping his voice down.

"How's that, Ed?"

"A trick I taught her this morning. Now you better

get moving." He picked up a couple of logs and held them tightly against his chest.

"Mom worries about you out here all alone," one of the boys called over his shoulder as he walked away.

"She's got nothing to worry about, never did have."

A Shoe, a Fable ℘

THERE WAS AN OLD WOMAN who lived in a shoe
with many, many children who had been left on her
doorstep. Every night after she had tucked them in bed,
the littlest ones first in the soft hollows of the sole, then
the older ones in bunks, she knelt down and prayed for
each child in alphabetical order from Albert and Aline
to Zeek and Zoe, names she had given them since they
had arrived with none. Many a night she was so weary
she fell asleep on her knees and dreamed that her prayers
would come true.

The shoe stood on the edge of town in a field long
gone to weeds and wild grasses. Close by, a huge outcropping of black rock plunged into a deep ravine.

"That's a bad place. You must never play there," the
old woman told the children.

She did not tell them that girl babies, as well as orphaned and crippled infants were said to have been
abandoned there. Indeed, she suspected that those un-
wanted children left on her doorstep might have died
in the ravine had she not lived in a shoe nearby and

always been willing to love one more little one, however malformed.

However, as the years passed and her labors increased, she became discouraged. No sooner had one child grown old enough to go into the world than two took its place. She had hoped that one of them would return someday to share her burden. No one ever did.

While praying one winter night, she took a very hard line with God, enumerating each child's disabilities, all beyond her power to remedy. She had arrived at the M's, precisely at Maggie, who had such a squint she had trouble bringing food to her mouth, but the old woman was so exhausted all she could say was, "Please, Lord, Please." The wind driving the snow against the windows was the only reply.

She fell asleep and slept until she heard shouts, "Hurry. Come out and see."

Children rollicking in a meadow of spring flowers greeted her. Maggie was holding a handful of buttercups under the chin of little Sylvia. The twins – the old woman had named them Peter and Paul in her prayers – were romping like a pair of puppies in spite of their legs stunted by rickets.

That night, the old woman began her prayers with "Thank you for the meadow and the pretty flowers but please…" and she repeated the list of each child's deformity.

The next morning the shoe was silent and empty. From a window she could see an apple orchard ripening in the summer sun. Peter and Paul emerged from a stream to chase each other on strong straight legs while Maggie, a beautiful young girl, watched with a steady gaze.

At the joyful sight of all her children cured and happy, the old woman thanked the Lord and spent the day resting on her doorstep in the warm sun.

That evening when she came to put them to bed, she discovered that a goodly number of children were missing.

"We'll look for them tomorrow," Peter and Paul volunteered.

Early next morning the twins, Maggie and all the remaining children set out.

"Don't worry. We'll be back by supper time," Maggie promised.

When no one returned that evening or the next morning, the old woman did worry. By afternoon she was sick with worry.

"Perhaps they lost their way and fell into the ravine," she said to herself as she hurried as fast as her legs could carry her to the edge of the ravine.

Upon finding no trace of footsteps on the rough terrain she started down the slope grabbing hold of trunks of stunted trees to keep from falling. The air was sour like that from a stagnant well. Small avalanches of mud and gravel set off by her steps plunged noisily into the shadows. Now the descent dropped so steeply she crawled backwards on all fours like a toddler until the walls of the ravine narrowed to the point that she was able to straddle the gorge. She probed the darkness inch-by-inch with one foot in hopes of reaching a level bit of ground but there was nothing, only more darkness and somewhere a black fissure cut into the earth.

Unable to go any further she had no choice but to retrace her steps. On the way, she stopped to scrutinize the damp ground and coarse thickets for signs: a child's cap left on a rock, a little glove caught in a bramble bush, anything she might not have noticed on the way down. She saw nothing, heard nothing except a faint echo in answer to her call, "Maggie, Peter, Paul."

And yet in the stillness, everything stirred as if set in motion by her presence. Dead leaves driven in a sudden updraft, scattered overhead before falling again. Starved vegetation and rocks wavered in the shadows of a shifting, unstable landscape.

She paused and looked back into the ravine. Suddenly, where there had been only darkness, lights flickered, little tongues of light elusive as fireflies, golden as tiny bees streamed out of the depths. She heaved herself out of the ravine, a bright swarm in her wake.

The shoe was empty. Not one of those who had left with Maggie and the twins had returned. She left the front door open just in case someone came during the night and then went to bed.

A pleasant sound like the whir of small birds' wings or the hum of sleepy voices filled the shoe and lulled her to sleep.

In the morning, she discovered the newcomers, soft little spirits who hid in the shoe's many nooks and crannies and filled the silence with their wordless murmuring.

In the days that followed, others came, always at dusk, bright and dancing out of the darkness of the ravine. In the evenings, since they were too young for the bed-time stories she had told her lost children, she sang them lullabies and for awhile put aside her weariness.

Occasionally, strangers came to the door, women with despair in their voices, asking, "Have you seen my baby girl? My little boy? He is blind."

The old woman felt sorry for these mothers living with the nightmare of having left their babies to die in the ravine but there was nothing she could do. The infant souls, unwilling to be reborn, made themselves invisible until the mothers went away. Then they came out of hiding and clustered around the old woman in a rosy band. They drew her into their simple, airy games and teased her so sweetly that she floated free of her aged self with its burden of sadness.

With the coming of winter, the shoe rested under a dome of ice-glazed snow that filtered the sunlight so that everything within was bathed in a silver twilight.

The little ones grew increasingly transparent and drowsy. With them she dozed through days and nights.

One morning she was awakened by a loud tapping. There in the kitchen window were Peter, Paul and Maggie, a beautiful young woman who held a white poodle in her arms. The twins had grown blond beards and fine, thick hair. Each carried a brief case.

"Please open the door," Paul called.

"We want to come back," Peter said.

"We are homesick," Maggie said.

When they received no reply they pressed against the window pane and Paul asked, "Can you see her in there?"

"No, but I do hear something, a humming like that in a hive," Maggie replied.

The old woman felt sorry for them. They looked as forlorn as when she had picked them up off her doorstep. That look had faded only after years of her care. Now they appeared tearful as the ice melting on the glass seemed to streak their cheeks.

"Please take us back," their eyes pleaded.

The old woman sighed, unable to tell them that there was no room for them in the shoe.

When Maggie said, "We will come back in the spring," the little ones flew circles in the silvery air whispering, "In the spring we will go home, go home, go home."

In the warmth of spring the little souls and with them, the old woman, grew lively and bright while under the melting snow the shoe shrank and shrank.

True to their word, Maggie and the twins returned as promised but they could find no trace of the old woman or the shoe.

While they stood bewildered in the field where they had once played, Maggie pointed to the sky saying, "Look. I heard them when I was here before."

The twins looked up but the sun was so strong they caught only a glimpse of brightness before it disappeared in the sunlight.

Stone

OUT OF FIRE AND ICE I came into the world, a stone.

One day I struck my brother in anger and fled into the wilderness.

Discovered by stone people, I was venerated as a sacred talisman possessed of magic powers. Worshipped, anointed with blood, I grew powerful.

After a period of glacial and volcanic violence, the world emerged from darkness. In the new spring light I was found in a marble quarry by a sculptor.

He loved me and said, "You are beautiful. I will cut away the coarse exterior and reveal your soul."

Of course, in the eyes and hands of any artist all materials : wood, clay, iron, have lovely souls.

I have a stone soul. It quickened at his touch but before he could reveal it he was struck down, killed by my blow.

I am not beautiful. He was my brother.

Secrets ✑

WE GREETED the great-aunts Sophie, Ottolie, and Matilda with a frightened stare when they arrived at Gran's house in a chauffeured black stretch limo. After bowing in order to step out, they stiffened straight up as if pulled on wire and stood so tall we could see the undersides of their sharply pointed chins.

"My dear sisters, I thought you'd come in a hearse," Gran said, waiting to greet them on the front steps. "A bad joke on my eighty-fifth."

The great-aunts tilted their faces under black hats with veils in order to kiss Gran on her cheek.

"Happy birthday, Maud," they murmured one by one. On their way into the big stone house of their childhood they noticed us on the steps.

"Look here, our little namesakes," Great-Aunt Sophie called to her sisters and blew kisses from her gloved hand.

We shivered in the sweep of violet blue eyes. The names weighed on our spirits. In secret we answered to Soph, Ott and Tilda.

The great-aunts always told everyone how much they truly loved us, how like them we were already, not only in name but in what they saw in our futures: beauty, brilliance and a lot of scary sounding *joie de vivre* happenings. Although they were old, they were strong, determined. They made things happen; the birthday party, for example, in what they called "the castle of their childhood." It isn't a castle, just a big house with lots of chimneys and a tower. They grew up there and Gran still lives in part of the house. We were afraid they really could make our lives happen their way. Their kisses and expectations hid a need we couldn't satisfy, a strange hungering that haunted their blue eyes.

That evening the house was crowded. The great-aunts insisted on having their old bedrooms so they could sleep "in the beds and dream the dreams of their youth." Regular aunts, cousins, grouchy in-laws wandered along dark hallways, up and down backstairs and into dead-end passages of locked closet doors in search of a place to sleep.

As the youngest guests we were assigned cots in the attic. From the third floor landing Gran pointed to a steep stairway.

"I can't make it up those stairs so haven't been up there for sometime but I'm sure…."

Great-Aunt Matilda broke in breathlessly, "Spending the night in our old playroom, you lucky things. What special times we had, remember, Maud?"

"Never mind, Matilda," Gran answered sharply and left us alone to climb the dark, narrow stairs.

Dolls all over the room, on the floor, on our cots, on the roof of their house, a large replica of the very house we were in, dolls lolled about, skirts up, bodices down, arms flung, legs spread in shocking attitudes even when part of a limb was gone or was suffering a seepage of shavings.

Young and inexperienced in the ways of the flesh though we were, even we sensed that something was going on – that warning "thou shalt not..." whispered by generations of mothers to daughters and here in this playroom under the eaves it had been going on for ages. We were surrounded by brazen creatures mocking the pretty, proper little girls who loved them and in pictures on the walls still held them tenderly. In time, those arms abandoned them. The pretty, proper girls tossed them aside in favor of hot-blooded lovers who crept into this attic playroom to play secret games.

The china cheeks still blushed, the rose-bud lips were pursed in tight knowing smiles and the lolling limbs burlesqued the games they learned, the play their innocent glass-blue eyes witnessed.

We were tired, uneasy far away in an attic room full of strangers. "It's bed time. On to your shelves, into your house," I said firmly and with Ott and Tilda saw that they composed themselves for the night.

For solace we pulled our cots together.

"Let's have the light on," Ott said placing the only lamp in the room, a rickety metal bridge lamp with a torn shade, at the head of our cots.

Once in bed, we lay isolated on a tiny island of weak

light under the blackness that descended from the high-pitched ceiling. And while the walls receded into darkness the glint of an eye, a pale thigh severed from its torso by the shadows, told us we were not alone.

In the morning we found them, well, you will have foreseen, slumped limply, half-asleep. During the night they had returned to their old ways and then from the shadows they observed us warily through half-closed eyes waiting for us to leave their room.

"Happy birthday, dear Maud, happy birthday to you," the great-aunts chanted as they and Gran hovered over the large, round, white cake at the head of the dining room table.

In the golden candlelight their faces grew smooth, young. Gran went on humming "Happy Birthday" to herself.

Great-Aunt Ottolie clapped her hands for attention. When the crowded dining room quieted she announced, "My sisters and I get one wish and you three girls," she pointed to us on the opposite side of the cake, "you get a wish."

Gran plucked three candles off the cake and handed one to each of us.

"First, these three beautiful, well-behaved children each get a candle to grow on."

My candle burning crookedly dribbled wax on my palm. Tilda's went out but Ott's burned steadily.

The great-aunts and Gran huddled together to settle on a wish. Excited as small children they whispered, giggled into their hands, and sent mischievous glances across the glowing cake at us. We wished we were invisible.

"Now we will all count to three and the birthday girl will blow out the candles," Great-Aunt Matilda ordered.

"Bravo," the regular aunts, cousins and in-laws shouted at the far end of the table.

Tiny spirals of smoke rose from the spent candles making the great-aunts' blue eyes water. Their faces suddenly hardened in the electric light but they laughed and chattered as gaily as girls.

"Oh, that was fun. We could light the candles and do it again," Great-aunt Sophie said and wiped her brimming eyes with a lace handkerchief.

"What did you wish?" someone behind us called out.

Great-Aunt Matilda flung out her arms in an exuberant gesture as if to embrace the whole room, the whole house in the wish "to be the way we were, beautiful and in love in this place of our youth." Smiling, she turned to her sisters whispering, "Remember when we...."

Their voices joined in a quiet laughter. Blue eyes passed a sly look from one to another and then suddenly fixed on us.

"And what did you girls wish?" Gran asked, her wrinkled face severe.

We stood blinking, our breath trapped in our throats.

"Tell us," all the great-aunts commanded.

We backed away from the table but could not escape the eyes. Finally I spoke up.

"It's a secret."

"Oh my, so you have secrets already. Hear that everyone. These young things are not as simple as they look."

Gran's tone was biting.

"Secrets already," the great-aunts echoed angrily.

A tense silence fell on the room until Tilda raised her hand. When she wants to, she can sound as sweet and plaintive as a fledgling in spring.

"Aren't you going to cut the cake, please Gran dear?" she asked.

Everyone in the room clapped to "Gran cuts the cake, Gran cuts the cake" as Great-Aunt Matilda handed her a sharp knife.

Boy ✍

THE BOY REMEMBERED that when he was little they had called him Oscar and he had called them Mom and Dad. He hated Oscar and had said so.

"We'll call you Boy," his mother had said.

Later, quite on his own he quit using Mom and Dad and began calling them Roy and Donna. They hadn't objected, hadn't noticed.

"Everything I do is okay with them," he told his friend, old Mr. Chavez who lived across the hall.

"Well then, no problems," Mr. Chavez said, offering him a Coke.

But he did have a problem. His mother lied and lied mostly about him.

She had always made things up. "Exercising my imagination" she called it. Then one afternoon he came home from school to find her pacing around the small apartment, kicking the legs of the tables and chairs and sobbing. The corner where Roy displayed his Viet Nam war memorabilia was empty.

"The war hero has dumped us here in L.A. He's gone to San Diego," she shouted over the blaring radio.

The boy had been to San Diego once with Roy to visit a battleship. The distance from Los Angeles wasn't all that great so, he suggested, maybe Roy hadn't dumped them, maybe he wanted to visit the marinas and all the u.s. Naval and Marine Corps bases in the area. She didn't see it that way.

"Use your imagination," she screamed on her way to the phone to call her girlfriend, Ann.

In the six weeks since Roy's departure his problem had increased. Her lies came out of nowhere, buzzed around him, stinging like hornets.

This afternoon Mrs. Giordano, seated on the stoop of the apartment building, had stopped him. "Good for you, Boy. Head of your class your mother tells me."

"And next year captain of the baseball team," Mrs. Wakowski chimed in from the doorway.

"Yeah, well not really," he mumbled and brushed past them.

He longed to blurt out the truth. "I'm a c+ student, b– athlete, not going to be captain of anything," but to deny her stupid stories would make her look bad so he sort of went along, all the while hating her lies and himself.

Although the door to the apartment on the third floor was closed he could hear Donna's flip flops slap the bare floor as she paced the living room. These days she was always edgy when she came home from Casa Margarita where she worked as a bar hostess. She would complain to him, "Tacky place, tacky customers, L.A. jocks in their running shorts and year around tans."

He opened the door with a key he kept on a key chain with a plastic silver dollar, one of Roy's presents for his thirteenth birthday.

"That you, Boy?" she called from the bathroom.

"Yeah, head of the class, captain of the baseball team. That's me."

"Don't be angry, dear. I'll be out in a minute and we'll talk."

He sat down in Roy's armchair. The room was hot and noisy, street noise from the open windows, radio noise from where ever she was. She enjoyed noise. Dead air, empty space depressed her. She liked things, china figurines, glass animals on every shelf, spider plants on the window sills. Roy had commandeered some shelves and wall space for his Viet Nam war trophies, framed maps, photos and ribbons mounted on black velvet. Now they stayed on like ghosts, their dusty grey outlines haunting the space they had occupied. Donna had covered the rest of the walls with travel posters of Bali, Alaska, Antarctica.

"And why do you think we can't go there? Dream the impossible dream," she exclaimed in answer to his doubts.

He could dream a lot of things but he knew what was real and what was not. Remote beaches and frosty blue glaciers weren't anymore real than Roy, a salesman for Global Airconditioning Inc., becoming, according to her, CEO of the company. Sometimes he and Roy teamed up to tease her about her impossible travel dreams.

Prompted by Roy he would ask, "How come we don't

have a poster of your Lake Baraboo, clean air, sweet water?"

In answer Roy would do a little song and dance routine, "Donna's Lake Baraboo, no place on earth like you, because there is no Baraboo."

This always got a rise out of Donna. After attempting to ignore their antics, she would break down and rush out of the apartment in tears.

Once she kept her temper, although her voice shook. "Look here, Boy." She spread a pile of photographs on the living room card table where he had to do his homework because his room was too small for a desk. "This is me and Gran." She handed him a photograph of a little blonde girl smiling in the lap of a white haired woman seated by a lake. "Here is another view. The pines around the lake. I used to play in the woods. Me with an armful of pine cones for the fireplace. The nights were cool. That's the little town of Trago in the distance."

Many of the photos were more or less the same, lake, trees, sky, but Donna didn't seem to notice. A shadow, a change in the surface of the water, a crow in the sky, all held her attention. "See how beautiful, you can feel how pure the air is," she repeated in a hushed voice as if she were actually in the pine scented landscape.

"Yes, I see," he answered and for the moment could feel the cool.

Thereafter he never joined Roy in joking about Lake Baraboo although he had his doubts. He had checked an atlas in the school library. Trago and the lake appeared as tiny dots on the map of Wisconsin but that didn't prove that Lake Baraboo was "really and truly Paradise" other than in Donna's fantasy.

These past six weeks with all her lies, he didn't trust anything she said and yet when in moments of depression she would reach out to him saying, "Some day, Boy, you and I are going to get out of this stinking city. We'll go to the lake where the water is as clear as the sky and the air is cool."

At such moments he believed in her and in the beauty of that place.

"I'm coming, Boy," she called from the bedroom.

He stood in the center of the living room angry and ready to face her.

"How was school?" she asked coming into the room wearing a pink terry cloth robe and carrying a small portable radio, silent at the moment.

"School was lousy. I flunked a math test and I wish you wouldn't...."

"I know, dear." She came over and kissed him on the cheek. "I love you. I love to praise you."

"Praise me," he exploded. The card table, hit with a pile of school books, shuddered. "Your lies make me feel weird, like I was somebody else."

His sudden fury startled her.

"All right, so let's not make a big deal out of two little fibs." She put her arm around his shoulders. "While I'm washing the chili smell of Casa Tacky out of my hair you figure out what to send out for, Chinese or pizza, for supper."

She ran her hand through her hair, her long red nails

flashed like tiny fish in and out of the blond curls. She smelled of too many margaritas, but his anger now turned inward. He couldn't speak.

She drew herself up and placing one hand on her hip, the other behind her head said, "After a shower I'll be sugar and spice and everything nice."

As she minced her way to the bathroom he rushed out of the apartment.

Mr. Chavez' door was ajar.

"Come in," the old man said looking up from his paper.

The boy sat down in his usual chair opposite Mr. Chavez, the open window between them.

"Want the sports page?"

"No thanks, I'm okay."

He stared out the window. The littered streets, empty warehouses and gutted apartment buildings, sunk in a wash of grey haze, appeared far away while the room with its white walls and meager furnishings floated quiet and airy above.

Mr. Chavez folded his paper so gently it hardly rustled in his hands. "Bad day?" he asked.

Still staring out the window the boy answered in a tense voice. "She's driving me crazy with her…" He hesitated to say "lies."

"With her stories," Mr. Chavez volunteered.

"Yeah, nutty stories like I'm wonder boy, son of Superman and the Bionic Woman." His throat tightened as he tried to laugh.

Mr. Chavez got up from his chair and returned from the kitchen with two Cokes in plastic tumblers.

"You've heard some of the stuff she makes up," the boy said.

"She misses your father."

"I miss him too but her inventing stuff doesn't help. Besides when they're together they're The Honeymooners."

Mr. Chavez looked puzzled. He only watched the Spanish language channel but the boy knew that given the cheap construction of the apartments his parents' angry voices reached the neighbors. The voices were not always angry. Sometimes they told jokes and laughed. Often the voice was Roy's telling of his exploits during the Viet Nam war. On Saturday afternoons when Donna went to the mall with Ann, Roy in his corner with his trophies and a six pack on the floor beside him was ready to talk about his war. Tet, Haiphong, Camranh, Hue, Da Nang, Mekong, Search and Destroy drive, body count, Free Fire zones, and the acronyms DMZ, NLF, MAF. The boy had learned them all, had heard most of Roy's talk before and yet he always found new thrills as he followed Roy through jungle green shadows, the air heavy with heat and humidity clinging to his skin like wet gauze, each step on the trail a step into danger from ambush, mines, traps studded with bamboo spikes sharp enough to penetrate an Army boot. But it was in the underworld of the Iron Triangle that Roy was most heroic. The boy could see the sixty-three square miles of ordinary jungle, paddy fields, villages as it looked from a helicopter.

"We had to go in," Roy said. "The Iron Triangle was

a Viet Cong stronghold, a dagger pointed at the heart of Saigon."

The boy agreed. He was ready.

"You remember the village Ben Suc, the v.c. control center of the Triangle. Ben Suc was really two villages, one you could see above ground, the other hidden below ground in miles and miles of tunnels."

Remembering Ben Suc the boy felt his gut tighten. Someone had to crawl into a hole leading down into total darkness.

"They called for volunteers. They needed small athletic aggressive guys. I was among the first to volunteer but I was a little too tall. Those stinking tunnels were narrow and low. However given my experience in hand to hand combat I guess they figured my aggressiveness compensated for my height and I became a tunnel rat. We worked in teams of six to ten guys."

Roy pointed to a photograph on the shelf of a slender man squeezing out of a hole in a plantation of rubber trees. His naked torso and face were blackened with dirt.

"No, it's not me, one of my team," he said.

The boy joined the team, got down on all fours and steeled himself. To go into that dark hole headfirst, armed with only a flashlight and a pistol took courage. Roy, the point man, went first.

"Those stinking winding tunnels went on for miles. At every turn there might be a v.c. hiding in the dark, shit, more than one. You couldn't see or hear them but they could sure hear us and spot the flashlight. Then there was the danger of booby traps. That was bad but remember…"

The boy shuddered. His stomach churned.

"Yeah," he gasped, "the bats and scorpions. No room to move. One of the team got panicky when the bats came at us."

"On the last day a section of tunnel collapsed just behind us. God damned bulldozers of the First Engineer Battalion of the First Infantry were knocking down the village houses. They could have buried us alive and never known it. We almost suffocated from all the dust and crud in the air. At last I found an exit and led us out."

The boy took a deep breath but it caught in his lungs. The air was dense with smoke, the burning village racked with the roar of helicopters, trucks, "tankdozers" searching for land mines.

"Mission completed." Roy reached over and slapped the boy on the thigh. "In record time without losing a man."

"Yeah," the boy agreed wishing he could talk as well as Roy so he could say how much he looked up to him, but all he said was "Yeah, you sure did it."

Together Roy and Donna tended to be loud. Once when they had been especially noisy, first arguing about money, then making up with tickles and squeals between kisses, the boy had tried to quiet them.

"The neighbors, Mr. Chavez, everyone can hear everything."

Donna had responded by doing her flamenco, much

wiggling of hips, stamping of feet and snapping of fingers. However Roy had turned serious suddenly and sitting down with the boy at the card table had said, "Tino Chavez fought in the Pacific, World War Two against the Japs. He was a hero in Bataan, one of the few survivors of his unit of the Bataan Death March. You ask him to tell you about it. Our guys took a terrible pounding but they got a lot of Japs before they were forced to surrender."

The boy found it hard to imagine Mr. Chavez killing anyone, but the Bataan Death March was vividly real on a large map of the Bataan peninsula that jutted from Manila Bay into the South China sea. With a magic marker, Mr. Chavez had drawn a red line from the southern end of the peninsula to a point ninety miles to the north. At intervals he had placed black crosses.

"Mis compañeros."

"My father, he's a Viet Nam vet and a hero, say's you're a World War Two hero. What did you…"

"No heroes, only survivors," Mr. Chavez had said sharply and whenever he was asked about the war he would either change the subject to baseball, his favorite sport, or withdraw into himself. Then the boy would notice him staring at a large crucifix that hung on the wall next to the map. On a shelf beneath it a votive candle burned. In the flickering light of the flame the blood looked wet in the wounds of the tormented body.

"Gives me the creeps," Donna had exclaimed. She always sulked when he visited Mr. Chavez. "Why do you visit that old geezer?"

"He's my friend. Roy says he's a war hero."

"Roy," she sniffed.

"How about another Coke?" Mr. Chavez asked.

"Thanks but I'd better go back. Waiting makes her nervous and she…"

"Waiting's tough," Mr. Chavez said.

The boy remembered Roy saying "Those poor bastards outgunned, outmanned and half starved waited and waited on Bataan."

He left Mr. Chavez seated, his eyes fixed on the map.

As he reentered the apartment Donna was talking on the phone with her divorced girlfriend, Ann. When she saw him, she put her hand over the mouthpiece.

"There's another postcard for you from Roy. It's on the kitchen table."

In the six weeks he had been away Roy had sent him several postcards of historic carriers, submarines, battleships, the sea and air around them filled with exploding shells. He had replied once with a goofy card of Charlie Chaplin in an ill fitting uniform, a rifle upside down at his side. Perhaps Roy with his ribbons and medals had missed the joke. He didn't reply.

"Oh Ann, I don't know which way to turn," Donna in tears was saying.

From past experience the boy knew she had forgotten about supper and would be on the phone for ages. He made a couple of bologna on rye sandwiches, ate one and wrapped the other in foil for the trip.

In San Diego it took him a while to find 125 Eucalyptus Street, the address Roy had given on his last postcard and once there he hesitated at the bottom of the steps that led up to the house. White stucco with faded blue trim, it stood in a row of similar houses on a grassy bank above the sidewalk. It had a solid, old fashioned air, not the sort of place Roy, who liked motels with cable TV and swimming pools, would choose. A porch ran across the front so that the house looked down from its green embankment with a wide smile. After checking the address on Roy's last postcard the boy started up the steps.

"Hi there."

The redhaired woman on the other side of the screen door was as smiling and solid as the house.

"Is Roy Walton here?"

"Sure thing. Come on in." She opened the door and called "Roy" up a wide dark stairwell. Then she went down the hall to the back of the house.

A dishwasher began to hum.

"Is that you, Boy?" Roy tousled and sleepy eyed, peered down. "Come on up, pal."

The boy, suddenly ill at ease, wandered around the bedroom. At the back of the house, it overlooked a sunny yard and vegetable garden enclosed by a hedge with scarlet flowers. The woman who had met him at the door was bent over weeding around a row of cabbages.

"How'd you get here?" Roy asked slumped on the edge of the unmade bed.

He looked pale and thin, more like the picture of him in uniform, now on the chest of drawers, than the bulky man the boy had always known.

"I took the bus. I was going to hitch but then I remembered you once told me never to do that. I'm sorry I didn't let you know I was coming. Things got kind of crazy in L.A."

Roy seemed about to say something but the boy was determined to finish what he had rehearsed on the bus.

"Donna misses you a lot. We both do. She wants you to come home."

Roy nodded and getting to his feet said, "Guess you'll be spending the night."

"I can sleep on the floor or in this armchair."

"Hell, no. It opens out." The boy helped Roy clear the floor around the chair of shirts, socks and newspapers.

"Presto pronto," Roy said.

The chair unfolded to a cot.

"I'll ask Beth for some bedding. She's the red head. A great gal. Her husband Bert is an old buddy of mine."

"Sorry for all the trouble."

"No sweat. I'll be right back."

While he waited the boy noticed a number of Roy's war mementos, an empty shell, bayonet and ribbons, half hidden by socks in an open drawer.

Roy returned with an armful of pillows and sheets.

"I was afraid you'd be gone when I got here, maybe on an out of state job," the boy said as he helped Roy make up the cot.

"Things are kind of slow right now."

Roy plumped up a pillow with such force a few white feathers popped out. Then clutching the pillow to his chest he asked, "Hey, are you hungry?"

"Sort of."

"Okay, we're off." He tossed the pillow onto the cot, grabbed a khaki shirt off the bed and put it on over his t-shirt. "There's a Taco Bell down the street."

At six o'clock the Taco Bell was crowded but the blonde cashier greeted Roy by name and pointed to an empty booth in the back. Although the boy felt hollow with hunger, he suddenly lost his appetite. The bright noisy atmosphere reminded him of Donna, of her half-asleep calling after him when she found his note that morning.

Roy had found friends in the booth across the aisle. The boy ate alone mechanically and then was very, very tired.

When he woke the next morning he found a note from Roy on the mirror above the chest of drawers saying "See you later. Help yourself in the kitchen."

The kitchen was a large sunlit room at the back of the house and like Roy's bedroom it looked out onto the garden.

"Morning," Beth said coming in from the back yard holding the ends of her apron loaded with vegetables. "There's milk and juice in the fridge."

As she emptied her apron onto the kitchen counter cherry tomatoes escaped from the pile to roll every which way like so many pinballs. He joined her laughing and grabbing them before they fell to the floor.

"How about some scrambled eggs?" she asked putting corn bread and honey on the kitchen table.

"No thanks, this is great."

"What do you usually have for breakfast?"

"Oh, whatever's in the fridge or a Snickers bar if I'm late. I keep a supply in the fridge so they're always fresh." Then noticing the look in her eyes he added, "Sundays, Donna, she's my Mom, makes waffles, all different kinds, but mostly chocolate."

"I see."

After refilling his glass of milk Beth began sorting the vegetables on the counter into baskets.

"What time does Roy come back from work?" he asked.

"All depends."

"Like on what?"

"Luck, dogs, the ponies." She looked up and facing him added, "Don't you worry. Your Dad will come back for you."

From the sound of footsteps half heard through sleep the boy was aware that Roy came and went at night. During the day Beth remained a smiling steady presence, always busy planning for Bert's return.

On the third morning she said, "You're waiting. I'm waiting. I sure could use some help in the garden. My Bert, he and your Dad are old friends, does a lot of the heavy work but while he's been on the road the weeds have been growing like," she shrugged and then laughing said, "just like weeds."

After breakfast he went with her into the garden. As they walked along the beds the only vegetable he recognized was corn.

"Carrots, beets," she explained pointing to the different foliage. "That wonderful looking stalk is brussels sprouts."

Her enthusiasm surprised him.

"I ate some once at school," he said to be polite.

She caught on immediately and said, "I guess once was enough for you."

They walked into a cool, shaded area where she grew lettuce. The varieties amazed him. Occasionally Donna made a Greek salad with olives, feta cheese and pale tasteless lettuce leaves. Here in small sections of a row were chicory, romaine, radicchio and a green that looked like a dandelion leaf.

"I just try to grow a little of each. This isn't an ideal climate for lettuce. Now over here is where I need your help. Bert's cabbage patch." She walked over to an area entirely planted in cabbages and stood hands on hips surveying the plantation. "These big fat cabbages hogging all this space and ready to take over the world are Bert's passion."

The boy agreed to do the needed weeding, especially because it was easy to tell cabbages from weeds. He would have felt uneasy with spinach.

At the end of the day she came over to inspect his progress.

"This is wonderful, Boy. You're a super worker. I can't believe you've never worked in a garden before."

The next morning he got up at sunrise. The garden was very quiet except for the sound of a faint sea breeze in the eucalyptus trees that grew beyond the hedge. It must have rained during the night. Every green and growing thing shimmered in the first sunlight. In the birdbath filled to overflowing he saw his face floating in a brilliant sky.

He set to work among the cabbages. The weeds came out easily from the damp soil.

"Breakfast, Boy," Beth called.

As he entered the kitchen she said, "Your Dad phoned last night after you had gone to sleep."

"Is he okay?"

"Sounded great. Said things were going really well and he'd be here for supper. I expect Bert home too, so we'll have stuffed cabbage and cole slaw."

The boy didn't see much of Beth for the rest of the day. She was out shopping and then busy in the kitchen while he was determined to finish weeding the entire cabbage patch. Once Roy returned he figured they would go back to L.A. together, surprise Donna, celebrate. She could do her flamenco.

"Smells terrific," the boy told Beth as they sat at the round table in the dining alcove off the kitchen.

"It's Bert's favorite but he and your Dad better get here pretty soon. I turned off the oven an hour ago."

She rearranged the knives and forks again at the two empty places. He drank another glass of water and ate a saltine.

"Waiting is hard," Beth said looking out the picture window at the garden now steeped in shadows.

"Yeah," he agreed.

Suddenly she roused herself.

"That cabbage can't wait any longer." She went to the stove.

Although dead tired from the long hours working in the garden, he slept fitfully, waking often to listen for Roy. Finally he fell soundly asleep. When he woke the bedroom was full of sunlight. Through the open window he heard Beth say with a tease in her voice, "I'll bet you had more than one for the road. Drink your coffee."

"Bert, this is Roy's son and Boy, this is my husband who's just got in."

Bert, a large man with spiky black hair, sat slumped in a chair.

Beth smiled as she stood behind him, her arms crossed on his chest.

The boy shook hands and then sat in his usual place. Breakfast was already on the table.

"Been driving all night. It's sure good to be home," Bert said rubbing his bloodshot eyes.

The boy heard a slur of fatigue and alcohol in his speech.

"Boy's been helping me in the garden." Beth sat down beside Bert, who put his left arm around her waist while he held his coffee mug in his right hand.

"You've got some super cabbages," the boy said and then concentrated on dripping honey on a piece of corn bread. He wanted to ask Beth about Roy, but she was so taken up with Bert, so happy to have him beside her chasing bacon and eggs around his plate with his free hand, that the boy felt embarrassed even being there, let along asking if Roy had phoned again, was he coming and when?

"Boy's weeded the entire patch in no time, and I've made enough coleslaw for four with plenty left over."

"Great," Bert said. "By the way, where the hell is Roy?" He looked around the kitchen as if to discover Roy in hiding.

"He'll probably be here by supper time. He knows Boy's waiting."

"'Boy,' that's a weird name."

From across the table Bert gave him a boozy look.

"It's a good name," Beth said quickly. "Roy's been delayed. He's on a roll, had a run of real luck."

Bert yawned, stretched his arms above his head and said, "Roy always was a lucky so and so."

"Bert and your Dad were in the service together," Beth said.

"Hell, Beth, I was in the war. Lucky Roy was in Saigon behind a desk. Never got off his butt while this stupid bastard was risking his ass. Tet, Hue, Da Nang…"

The boy sat stone still. Camranh, Me Kong, NLF, MAF, Cedar Falls Search and Destroy. The names were so deeply fixed in his mind that he no longer heard Bert, only Roy's voice. "Tet Hue Da Nang…"

"That's enough war talk. Come see the garden and then you need some sleep," he heard Beth say.

He watched them go arm in arm. Beth and Bert. Bert and Beth. He hated them for being alive, so happy there together among the cabbages. He hated them for knowing about lucky Roy. He wished they were dead.

As he made his way up the stairs to the bedroom he hurt. His ribs tightened, breath blocked, his lungs ached. Seething, he gasped. His eyes ready to burst with suppressed tears burned dry.

In the bedroom he quickly went through Roy's clothes. Roy was careless about small amounts of cash. The ash tray on top of the chest contained nothing but pennies. He searched the drawers. A glint of metal among the shorts caught his eye. Some of Roy's war trophies. He slammed the drawer shut and went to the closet. Frantic now for fear he couldn't get away before Roy returned, he grabbed clothes off hangers.

In the pocket of grey sweat pants he found a couple of crumpled dollar bills. Not enough for his bus fare to L.A. He knelt down to search the jackets and trousers fallen on the closet floor. Under a pair of red jogging shorts he uncovered the top to the sweat pants. As he pulled it out he heard something drop among the shoes. In the semi-darkness of the closet he found it, the metal clip with the American eagle that Roy used for five and ten dollar bills instead of a wallet.

I took just enough for bus fare home. Be a hero. Call Donna.

With the money clip he attached the note to Roy's picture of himself on the chest of drawers. From the window he gave a quick glance into the garden. The cabbages, silvery green in their sleek skin, looked up from their patch. Beth and Bert were strolling slowly toward the house. He left without saying goodbye.

Near the back of the bus the boy found an aisle seat beside a sailor wearing headphones and slumped, eyes closed, against the window. In the seats across the aisle a young woman sat with a little girl asleep next to her. When the driver came to collect the tickets she gave him a scared smile. He shrugged and looking down at the child said, "No charge for her."

After he moved on the woman kept on nodding and smiling down the aisle after him.

The landscape soon turned to desert, empty yellow hills traversed from crest to crest by enormous pylons supporting cables. Occasionally an irregular stretch of green appeared down in a valley, a pale cabbage green.

The boy, turning away from the view, took a package of jelly beans from his pocket. Across the aisle the little girl whimpered and sat up. She stared at him through thick glasses held in place by a red elastic band over her black hair. From time to time the heavy lenses caught flashes of sunlight reflected off the chrome of passing cars.

He offered her some bright orange jelly beans. The child peevishly twisted the skirt of her faded blue dress with both hands and ignored his outstretched palm.

"Her eyes," the mother explained pointing to her own. "In Tijuana the curandera promise me she be all right. We must wait."

The boy withdrew his hand, the pain working in him turning to rage.

As he approached the apartment building, Mrs.

Wakowski was stuffing a plastic sack of trash in one of the metal garbage cans alongside the stoop. The sack kept ballooning up over the edges of the can. When she saw him she stepped onto the sidewalk still holding the top of the can.

"I've been watching for you. Where you been?" she asked.

"Wisconsin. Pure air, no smog." Glaring at her he edged his way to the steps.

"Wisconsin, where in Wisconsin? That's not what your mother told me." Mrs. Giordano faced him from the doorway.

"Lake Baraboo. It's on the map. Clean water, pure everything if you want to believe it."

"What are you so angry for?" Mrs. Giordano called as he dashed up the stairs.

"It's me," he called from the living room so as not to startle her.

The living room furniture, card table, chairs, plant stand all stood at one end of the room as if waiting for something to happen. Nearby the Hoover lay flat on the floor.

"It's me," he called again.

"Oh, Boy, dear, you're back." She hurried into the room. She was wearing a blue chenille bathrobe. "I've just washed my hair. Too wet to kiss you." She blew him a kiss. Her cheeks were flushed, her eyes red under dripping bangs. "Just hold this for a minute." She handed him her drink and taking the towel off her shoulders wrapped it in a turban around her head. "There now," she took back the glass saying "Come sit down here by me."

Her bare feet left wet prints on the bare floor. He followed her to the furniture and sat down on a straight chair. A sudden hot gust of air pushed a lowered venetian blind into the room and then subsided, leaving the blind to fall back against the sill with the clatter.

"So tell me how was Roy?"

She took a swallow of the drink and then put the glass on the floor at her feet.

"He was okay, I guess."

"What do you mean you 'guess'?" She leaned her face close to his. "Did he say anything about coming home?"

The boy shifted in his seat away from her. She straightened up stiffly, and reknotted the belt of the robe.

"Well, tell me did he talk about coming home?"

The boy waited feeling the tension in her bore into him. Then he looked her in the eye. "Sure he talked about it. He's going to phone you."

She stood up and held out her arms.

He let her embrace him, her tears hot on his cheeks.

The phone rang in the kitchen.

"That'll be Ann. She was coming over for a drink. I'll put her off."

As he left the apartment he heard her say, "Boy's back from camping in Canada and Roy will be coming home any minute."

Mr. Chavez wasn't home. The boy sat down next to

the window and waited. Beneath the crucifix the candle had burned very low. The pointed flame in the glass holder was steady but tiny. On a table near his chair several paperback books about baseball were stacked in a neat pile and beside them an album, its white cover labeled in Mr. Chavez's handwriting "El Infierno." From a few rare remarks Mr. Chavez had made the boy knew the album contained a record of the Bataan Death March. Mr. Chavez had never offered to show it any more than he had been willing to talk about the war. On the other hand he had never forbidden the boy to ask questions nor had he kept the album concealed. It was there at hand.

On the opening page six pairs of eyes stared out of faces so emaciated he couldn't be sure if the men were alive or dead. Beneath each face was a Spanish name. One was Tino Chavez. The following pages contained more photographs of men in ragged uniforms, some wearing dirty blood-soaked bandages. Yellowed newspaper clippings read "Escaped Americans report Japanese atrocities. American P O W s beaten, bayoneted, shot to death on Bataan Death March." He turned to the final page where a small clipping stated "Sergeant Tino Chavez, survivor of Bataan Death March, returns home. Decorated for…"

A wrinkled brown hand closed the album preventing him from reading further. "You're back," Mr. Chavez said quietly. "Your mother worried."

"Sure she worried about me in Canada, Oregon, the outer galactic circle," the boy replied, his old anger surging. "I left her a note. She knew I was in San Diego with Roy." Saying Roy's name, hearing himself say it made him gasp. His eyes blurred with tears. He looked up into Mr. Chavez' wrinkled face. "Roy is a rotten faker fucking phony liar. Maybe he isn't even my father which is okay by me. He lies about everything. He says you are a war hero. You tell me the truth."

"No heroes in hell," Mr. Chavez said.

"Yeah, just survivors like you always say. Then tell me how you survived in hell."

The old man went slowly to the map of Bataan and tracing the red line from south to north with his forefinger stopped at the first black cross.

"My brother killed by American fire from Corregidor. The Japanese used us as shields. This cross is for Joe Romero, weak from dysentery. I carried him for awhile. When he couldn't keep up a soldier bayoneted him. Here April 12 near Balanga." Mr. Chavez tapped the spot. "They hacked four hundred of our men to death with their swords. No one ever knew why." He moved his finger further along to the next cross and then pulled his hand away. "This was terrible. Joe Hanks sick with malaria staggering on the cobblestone road. A guard pushed him in front of an oncoming tank. He went down. That tank followed by ten more rolled over him. In the end only a uniform was left, part of the cobblestones. No man. They marched us over the spot."

Mr. Chavez' voice broke. He stood in silence, head bowed. Nearby the flame of the vigil light flickered erratically.

"The candle, it's about to go out," the boy said.

Mr. Chavez bent down and blew out the candle. Then, seated at the table, he began to remove the thin film of wax remaining at the bottom of the glass holder with his pocket knife. For a while concentrated on his work, he said nothing. The boy waited, his eyes fixed on the map. At the sound of the metal blade scraping the glass he flinched.

Mr. Chavez continued in a flat voice, "Before we surrendered we were half starved, fighting with one thousand calories and less in our bellies. No food, no medicine, nothing was getting through the Japanese blockade. Some of the men were barely able to climb out of their foxholes. We held on, defending our last line of defense. They kept coming. Then in the middle of the battle we heard reinforcements were on their way." He put aside the glass and knife and opening the album read "Help is on the way from the United States. Thousands of troops and hundreds of planes are being dispatched."

He closed the album and looking at the map said, "Those are the words of General Douglas MacArthur, January 15, 1942. We waited and waited, fought trapped in our own filth in stinking fox holes. On Good Friday the lines collapsed in chaos. We surrendered and the Death March north began, some sixty-two thousand Philipinos and ten thousand Americans."

"But MacArthur promised," the boy said.

Mr. Chavez' face was immobile in spite of the tears that glistened on his dark cheeks.

"There weren't any troops and planes on their way, never were any. No planes, no troops. It was a lie."

He placed a new candle in the glass. His hand trembled as he struck a match.

From across the hall Donna was calling, "Boy, Boy come back," or was she calling Roy? The boy couldn't tell. Drink blurred her voice.

He didn't answer.

Mr. Chavez placed the lighted candle on the shelf below the crucifix and watched for a moment to make sure the wick burned. Then he turned saying, "Forget trying to be a hero, Boy. Surviving with the rest of us is tough enough. Take it easy and after awhile…"

"After awhile what?"

"You'll grow bigger and be stronger than anyone's lies."

"Like a big fat cabbage," the boy said grimly through his teeth.

"Like a man." Mr. Chavez smiled and put out his hand.

THE NEW AMERICAN FICTION SERIES